Content Test (Novel)

By Rodrigo Haro

<u>This novel is dedicated to my Grandmother, my father and my niece</u>

Maria Santos Haro (August 1, 1912-January 2022), Jesus Perea (1941-?) and my niece Penelope Chanel Vitela (March 29, 2018- November 25, 2018).

Part I: Content Test

Chapter 1: Content Test

There's something in the activity of writing. There was something out of place in the environment. Something was egging him on. The day was getting by without trouble. God knew. His name was where he needed to be, he needed to get to our Side, the South Side. He was on the opposite, the North Side. He carried William Shakespeare on his side. *Twelfth Night.* He had to take it South.

He really needed to read, but his mind was somewhere else. He knew he had to write. He knew his texts were important to him. God, I need to write, he thought. He walked with texts in his hands without opening them.

He needed to get his address. He carried E.L. Doctorow's *Billy Bathgate.* He also carried an Illinois Licensure study book. The Content Test was to teach secondary education English. He needed to take it. He carried these texts on Broadway Ave. heading South. He knew he had to study.

He never got home. He made dinner staring at the Content Study book on his desk. He could not get to his desk. He kept flipping his steak over and looking at the small studio apartment. He could not get to his desk with his Content Test study book on top. The book laid on his desk. He tried to pass the Content Test three times.

He had tried to make it home, so many times only to go back North.

Most of his classmates had taken the Content Test. Some had passed it. Some had not. Most of his classmates at Northeastern Illinois University lived North. Some headed South. Some made it home to visit. Others lived in solitude. The Content Test was (superfluous) tedious, and so were his visits home. It was something he had to do. But never got to. Time and energy, he lacked. Adore the door. Make it home. He thought he knew the knowledge to pass the test, and make it through his mom's door. He had family issues.

He would stop talking to his mom for a couple of days. He would fall out of prayer, and fall out of communication. He would visit his mom sporadically, as well as study. Life is borrowed, not sold. My thoughts are sporadic, he thought. The words stuck with him, cunningly. A fierce reminder of normalcy. (He needed his destination, he just needed to get there). He needed to get to the door to be fulfilled, to achieve fulfillment. (There was something repetitive, redundant, and reliable about studying about the Content Test).

His visits were the same. He had visited his mom before without sentiment. At times it was climatic. Unappreciated at times. The same with the Content Test. He needed to try to figure out a strategy to conquer it, to get past his anxiety, to pass the Test, to pass through the doorway of his mom's house. He found his mom after two days of not seeing her. He called her on the phone. He had to let her know he loved her.

He needed to just think, to breathe, to just take action in prayer. To know he was in His presence. He wanted to socialize with whom he wanted to socialize with. He wanted to reconcile. He wanted to run home. He wanted to go back home. He needed to be in prayer. He needed to go back home. He needed to find his mom fast. He had to get her to South Chicago. He went all the way South, and turned back. He took the train and the bus for some time. He never made it home. He never took the bus. He turned back North. He missed the bus, and never took the next.

He struggled everyday to be by her side. That day, he tried to get to her right away. The trip from Rogers Park to South Chicago was far. He was dressed, and had coffee before the eighth o'clock train on the Red. He traveled fast. As soon as he thought he acted.

He took the train for two days. He never made the third try. He needed to get to 87th. The first day he turned at 47th. The second day at 35th. (There was a Sox game). He thought he would make it both times. He turned back in regret. The optimist in him told him that he would make it the day after. I made it a bit further, he thought.

He did not make it to her birthday. He was one block away. He waited at the bus stop for twenty minutes until he made up his mind and left. He thought about the Content Test less. He thought he would pass it just by taking it. He prayed and prayed for the Content Test.

The day of his mom's birthday, he turned back North twice on his way home. Time was bringing him back home, Time or God.The CTA worker on the 87th station didn't let him go through the turnstile. His anxiety got the best of him. He needed to get on the 87th bus and ride (or die) and go home.

He knew he was supposed to stay up the stairs waiting for the bus. His direction was the right direction. His direction was clear. Up the stairs and East. Instead he went down, up the stairs again and then West, going left.

He took the 87th bus West, a way away from his family. He did not know how to get back to his mom. He did not think of the Content Test. He thought about his mom, but could not get there. He left his North address, and came back and called his mom. He knew he was in the wrong address. He made sense of his disaster. He wanted to go back home. Jealousy leads to dependency, he thought to himself. He wanted to be. He talked to God. He prayed and all signs took him South. He prayed and wanted to leave the North. He stayed calm and ate. He felt guilt and anger.

He wanted to run to her. He felt danger without her presence. The Content Test was an entity he wanted to be kept alive, most dear to his heart. He needed to think of himself and be still. He needed not to be lost. He scheduled it for his birthday. He went through the South Side door and saw his mom, not fully aware of where things lay, but self-aware of his consciousness. Silence spoke immensely. He was there ready for another chapter of his life.

Chapter 2: Letting Go

The day he let go of Student Teaching for the second time he knew it felt right. The depression on that day was coming, and going. He thought of plummeting depression and the sentiment was not something he wanted in his mind. His health was his concern and he knew he could stay in (or, reach) wellness by just thinking. By just thinking differently. By his thinking of Cognitive-Behavioral Therapy. The way you think is the way you act. I can act differently, he thought, if I just think differently. (I shouldn't identify myself in the second person, he further thought). He thought about the abandonment he was committing. He thought about Mrs.

Henderson. He thought about the need to fulfill his destiny, he thought about his teacher, and the need to fulfill his promise to stay by her side.

These are doubts that are damaging. These thoughts are reassuring.

He thought about her unreasonableness, her unrelenting pursuit of her own will over his power. He thought about her unending following, showing her desire to just see him by her side. He felt relieved, stressed, and harassed. He would back off to breathe, to let her know he needed space, comfort to reassess. He would take a couple of steps back. She would follow him. Just follow him. She would not let him talk to other people, and would not let him have freedom movement.

She started to abuse him, asking him where he was, telling him where to go, and where not to be. She was like a human GPS to him. He was tired. He was stressed. She pursued a randomness bordering on catastrophe. She pursued disasters. She was always catastrophizing. She seemed to be guarding him against the harm of his own actions.

It's better to write in first person. I bless Destiny may she have a great Destiny.

The weaker part of me thought she was not thinking the best, but expecting the worst. Hope was only something she could only attain after sinking down into the hole. Or, so he thought. His pessimism, the creation of his own thoughts, created these scenes. Achievement only after catastrophizing, was one of his weakest thoughts. Why not just achieve now? A rebirth can be attainable. A new beginning. But also the loss of an experience. The end of something is hard. The start of something is harder.

The light for him was only to be found in the darkness. The switch had to be turned down when I kept thinking and telling her it doesn't have to be turned-off in the first palace. Calmness. Godliness.

He pictured an island of support. He thought about swimming away from the island. He thought about swimming from the island of support inhabited by all those he loved, showed him support, and he wanted to support. He thought about the island of inhabitants he lost and placed on the island, only for him to swim away in a small, paddle boat, looking back, looking from side to side, with only the sea by his side.

I have to find a way to be on the island, he thought. I have to be mindful. He was reading Macbeth by William Shakespeare. He thought about the plot, the writing, the thinking that the play instilled. The thinking made for unruly writing.

Chapter 3: Jaimie

There was a girl in South Chicago when he moved back after college. Her name was Jaimie. She was a friend from high school. Ten years ago. She was a sweetheart. She lived across the street from him on the block. She was married to his best friend from high school. His name was Georgie. The baby's name was Georgie Junior. She worked at Target. He worked in human services in a facility for people with disabilities.

He never said hi to her when he moved. He lived there less than six months. She never was home. He came home late. She was always at home. He could never catch her. He thought hard about going out and looking for her. She heard him knock once. She wasn't home.

She didn't want to open. She seemed violated, mistreated, and not taken cared of (ignored). He went to the store once to look for her. (He had visited her for breakfast. He walked out the door looking for work that day). He never wanted her at his house. (He trusted himself to let her in. She knocked once at least, he thought). He remembered vaguely how he showered instead of going to the door. She wanted to get back together with him. They were friends for life. He wanted to have sex, but never could relate.

He was removed from Student Teaching three weeks into the semester. He didn't get along with his Coordinating Teacher. For the second time, he left student teaching. He ran to his mom. He wanted to see her everyday.

One evening he showed-up at her door asking to get in. He was wearing his school clothes, and a tie, with his bag hanging from him. He clutched his shoulder strap strewn across his chest while he talked to her on the porch. He begged to get in while his neighbor wondered what he was doing, not going inside safely. She was his friend from childhood, from his teenage years, and could not get her to relate to him.

He did not like to be on the porch because it meant he wasn't going to go in. He took the opportunity to just talk to her. He saw her sporadically before then. He visited her every day now. She was (ironically not) happy with him. He was proud of her. He tried to get South everyday. She was constantly there for him, and struggled to see him now that he was away. She opened the door. She tried to have peace.

His removal from his office was voluntary and involuntary. It didn't matter. What mattered was the experience. He had another stint in teaching. Another piece of writing. He felt Present. He needed to stay present and live. He needed to just stay still. He needed to stay put. He needed to pray. No sudden action was needed.

The worse was over. He thought. Now to move South. His teaching responsibilities lay in the South. He needed to sub. That was his only choice. He needed to be a substitute teacher fast. He needed South.

What are we doing here? He thought as he stood on the porch staring at her (forced anger, anger not made to be there, anger that was unkempt).

"What are you doing here?" she asked as if answering his thoughts.

"I just came to see you," he answered.

He didn't know where to go, or what to do. She stared at him as if expecting something else. "We don't need trouble," he heard on the radio while listening to Bob Marley and the Wailers, "War/ No More Trouble." "We need love," the song went. He heard this days later while writing.

I don't need conflict, he thought. "I need love." He had his work bag with him. A study bag from school. "She told me to go home." Eric Clapton sang on the radio. There wasn't any anger, only confusion. He felt proud to be teaching again, only slightly erratic by his behavior and hers.

He went down the stairs to pray. Hitting the sidewalk he strolled, stepped to the bus stop on the parallel street, Commercial Ave. He felt kind of betrayed, but proud, satisfied that he visited her and got through his anxiety. He was part of society and had beaten anxiety. He crawled back into society without anxiety. He was proud he had gotten to his mom, yet he wanted to see his brother who he hadn't seen in days. He worked to eat with his mom and him. He wanted peace. He wanted to let her know he was following his dreams. He wanted to be proud of his mom for raising him right, and giving him the image to allow him to be a man. He wanted to show her the image of him following vision and teaching and succeeding. He needed to let her know he was okay.

The day he left the porch he thought why is my mom kicking me out. He needed to let her know he needed to stand. He needed to be there for her and show his face. He needed to let her know he could visit her. But she seemed to want to force conflict. She didn't understand that she didn't need to fight to get along.

He stood on the black porch.

"Why don't you let me in?" he asked.

"What are you doing here?" she responded.

We should not concentrate on questions, but answers, he thought. Why are you answering a question with a question?

"Pa verte," he responded.

"Why do you want to see me? She asked in Spanish.

"I'm just here to see you?" I answered.

She didn't respond, but kept telling me this. I couldn't go inside. I pleaded. But her answer was negative.

I stood there with my tie and collared shirt waiting to act, to act in praise. I prayed and prayed. I prayed. I didn't want to go down the stairs. I wanted to see my sister, and my nieces and nephews. I needed to make peace. I needed to just depart on good terms. I needed to make it indoors, and just stay calm. But she wasn't budging. I need to see my sister with her children, safe and sound. I needed to just stay still and be calm. She seemed to want to instigate and produce conflict. She seemed to be confused about her own abuse, wondering why she was fighting the son she loved. She seemed to be bewildered about the circumstances, the ones she was creating, and the ones she couldn't control.

I was dumbfounded, ecstatic that I was there, yet confused as well, confused about her confusion. I stared into her eyes knowing they showed love, yet also looking for an answer knowing that she didn't want to do what she was doing, knowing that she didn't want to leave me on the porch, knowing that she wanted to let me inside the house, our home. She was forcing herself to cause conflict, forcing herself to the darker side of things, the pessimism, the fake hatred (the avenue for any conflict that was forced). She was in the light looking for a way to create darkness. She was looking for any conflict to instigate a fight, thinking that fighting would create conversation which would lead to communication, calmness, care, endearment or unity. When God knows conflict creates conflict. Unity does not create conflict. God help me, he thought. You cannot create harmony out of conflict. The opposite of getting along is fighting. You cannot create White out of Balck. No matter how hard you try. The black is pitch black. The white, the light will slowly fade. Fade into black. Pessimism is hatred, hatred for self, for others, for humanity, hatred for understanding, hatred for compassion, hatred for empathy. All these things, empathy, compassion, love, are not created, and are not a product of blackness, or conflict, of fights, of misunderstanding, of apathy, or of hatred.

Apathy and misunderstanding lead to death. Lead to murder, lead to violence, lead to the opoosite of love. He believed their minds needed to understand that God and the power of will did not lie in darkness, where there is no Light. Getting along is not fighting. Fighting is not getting along. Getting along is getting along. Well. Let us be wiser. Let the stubborn die.

He walked away desperate for attention. Satisfied that he had visited her in prayer, yet wanting more. He had accomplished his goal of visiting her mother, yet he knew he had not fulfilled everything. He needed to be with her.

The porch was a huge non-prayer space. It was a space where he had been kicked out before, where he had been charged before, where the cops had looked for him. A space without praise. A space where he had been arrested before. It was a space in between praise. Either you're or you're out. Either I would go in for my visit and end my depression to fulfill my destiny to save my mom, or turn back, go down the stairs and just be a traveler. He needed to act fast. He needed to see her.

His students were some of his best students he had had so far. The most recent. There was one particular girl, a lonesome student, named Griselda Rios
I have to write everything else.

Chapter 4: Griselda Rios

She was in huge prayer. She was a huge blessing. She was late to school, she was late to start the semester (God let her stand-up and go home). I kept praying for her to come back, to just be present, to just come back. It was two weeks into the semester and she wasn't back. I prayed and prayed. God let Gabby come back to school. She showed up two weeks into the semester.

She was a huge blessing. Immediately, she gravitated towards me and I towards her. She was a huge blessing. I felt her soul connect to mine in a way that no one could understand. I felt her heart palpitate with every step she took. She was a bright student who I knew I had a deep connection with. Towards the end everyone wanted us to fall apart and be apart. They were forcing us to not be together. My Coordinating Teacher. I took her once to a therapist in the school. She needed to talk to someone about her academic difficulties. She seemed to fit in and wanted to feel safe, and be safe, at all times. She always wanted to be by my side to feel safety, Godliness, and a feel of pure safety.

She needed to feel safe and I always was, as much as I could, by her side. I need to just be with her, love her. She was someone who I didn't ignore, and who didn't ignore me. She needed to always stay positive in the light, and needed me (more than her) to feel the connection, to be by her side, to not feel fear, or danger, and feel a sense of togetherness. Although she was young, she was one of those persons who you never forgot and who you always looked her. She needed to be together with me. I needed to be together with her. It ended amicably. She got taken away because we talked and I offered support. She was instructed to sit in the back of the classroom during our free period which served as lunch. Usually, she sat in the front by the table by herself and approached me to talk, and I approached her to talk as well. After our amicable relationship, she got taken away and sat in the back with students who were picked for her to be her friends.

I loved her. I still do. I love her. As a fiend, student, and person.

Chapter 5: Sister's Birthday

On the day of my sister's birthday, I saw her at my mom's house. I went through the door with my sister's blessing. I knew I had to see them both, but especially my mom. I had to just be me and no one else. I had to see my mom, and my sister provided the occasion to see her. I had to just be there at home.

On my sister's birthday I went home. I went to my mom's house. I stayed there for a couple of hours.

She had stated earlier during the week that he could meet her at their mom's. He went to his address, his mom's, and saw her depressed. She was wearing jogging pants which seemed to be two days old. She was wearing an old shirt, white in color with designs. I wish she would have felt better. She was obviously saddened by my presence, saddened by the fact that she couldn't figure out how to lift herself up. She was obviously going through intense emotional abuse and trauma. I stayed there for a couple of hours when she left.

She went into the bathroom and put on make-up. A sign that she was getting ready for sex (whch to me meant that she was in danger of getting rape). My mom went into the bathroom with her, and shut the door. My sister said nothing. My mnom walked around her for a while in her private space (in the bathroom). My sister was obviously under psychological abuse. She was obviously being abused.

My mom shut the door without a word while my sister stayed in the bathroom. My mom obviously did not want to urinate and wanted to make a statement. She made her statement through

My mom opened the door after I heard the toilet flush. I saw huge non-praise on her face. I saw them communicate through silence. My sister, through silence, was accepting her abuse and silence. My mom was instilling something in her that day. She was saying, through silence, don't speak of what I'm doing. I felt like I had to corse silence,and not speak of what I was witnessing. I felt I was not going to be kept safe. She was obviously there to urinate. She was letting me know that it was weird, it was something uncommon, it was something unpredictable.

My sister spent countless hours in front of the mirror in the vanity, and the floor-length mirror on the shower doors behind her, looking at her eyes and putting on make-up. Hiding the scars that time had created. And hoping the new scars would not appear by wearing make-up. Hoping that the make-up would cover the upcoming sacrs.

He never understood. He didn't understand what was happening. He didn't understand the trauma that was happening, or the intense abuse that was happening. He walked-out after seeing her go. After losing her. She walked away from the address after putting on make-up, and I was left wondering why. She walked away from her own birthday celebration. I didn't go after her, but just left the address.

I left wondering where to go. SAFE. She left and then wondered where I was at. She left and I went outside to look for her. She left and I walked to the bus station confused by the acts without praise. I texted her back when I was at the bus stop waiting for my bus. She texted.

"When are you coming back?"

I answered, "I'm going home."

"Why did you leave?" she responded.

"I left because you left."

"Why don't you come back."

"I'll try to see you tomorrow," he responded.

"I was going to be right back," she texted back.

"I needed to elave. I thought you were going to stay," I responded.

I got on the bus. She tried to get me back to my jom to celebrate. She disappeared without telling me. She said she would be right back, and would. He forgave her.

He called and grew desperate to reconcile. He wanted to get things back the way they were. He needed to just be by her side. He needed to stay in prayer. He needed to know he was okay. He wanted to go home immediately as the thought entered his mind. There was no one who knew who he was. There was no other person who knew him best. He didn't pass the Content Test because he wasn't at home.

Chapter 6: God bless my dad, Jesus Perea. Eternal Rest Grant Unto Him and Let the Perpetual Light Shine Upon Him. Amen

Part II

Chapter 6; The Restaurant

My dad owned a restaurant when I was young in South Chicago called *Las Brasas*. He built it himself after retirement brick by brick. He raised us in the address. He was a man with an address. He made it big and opened up a restaurant. He needed to raise his kids right.

The restaurant lasted more than two years. My sister who is two years younger was raised there with me. I was five and she must have been three, twenty-three months months younger, when my mom became a single mom. My mom would run away with me by her side.

I was raised in the back of the address in an apartment in the back of the building. I was raised in the restaurant as well which was in the front of the building. I was raised in an out of the restaurant and the apartment in the back. When my mom worked, which seemed like ten hours a day. I was in the restaurant. I was running around and hoping to help. I must have been five. One time I took a plate to one of the tables. I asked my dad if I could serve the plate. I went from table to table looking for the people who ordered the plate. It was table one. I went to the other end of the tables set in the dining room. I went to the last table and ended up on the first. I asked every table on the way if it was their plate. Table one was on the other end. I owed myself better behavior. I knew it must have been on one or the other. It was an experience. My mom and dad watched behind the kitchen. They looked through the order window and saw me work my way through the tables. I felt I knew the restaurant. There must have been fifteen tables from one end to the other. I went to every table asking, "Is this your plate?"

I found the table on the other end. The last was first and the first was last. I saw the table of customers, a couple, looking over the table, the booth with leather benches and wood tables, from the other end. I looked up and kept gign to the nest table. When I finally got there, I had a feeling the food was cold, it must have been tacos, the meat seemed less hot. I got to the table and asked, "Is this table one?"

"Yes," the woman who looked directly at me said to me, shaking her head up and down. I put them down on the table and walked away. I turned my back, relieved that I had completed the task. I kept my honor. I walked away embarrassed, but hard-headed as I am, I looked forward to the next step.

I was hard-headed by not understanding that the table was on the other end. I needed to stay clear of the wrong path which encapsulated my stourbness. My mind told me that the table was at the end. Either one or the other. The table was one. I went through fifteen, fourteen, and twelve until I got to the other end. I had the wherewithal to go from table to table and ask them directly if that was their plate.

I had to just find the table and do nothing else. I felt embarrassed. I felt scandalized. I felt like I did not know my job, or better, that I was belittled by my own actions, to seem like I didn't know my place. My job, my restaurant.

I remember that I was strong in the restaurant. The image never leaves me. I did what I had to do to serve the food. I felt like I betrayed myself and my dad. My mom stayed silent. But I felt like I betrayed her as well. She knew my dad was going to scream at her, and blame her for her actions, instead of talking to me directly. Eye to eye. Man to five-year-old man. I felt like I had to hide.

I felt like I had done wrong by doing right. I had put down the plate, yet I had made a mockery of myself. By going table to table I redeemed myself when I got to the end table. I had to make my exit quick. I had to just get out of view fast. I had to hide and just know that I did my job. That I tried to do what I could. We had few customers that day and my mom and dad were the ones in the restaurant. There was a waitress on duty. She let me carry the plate, it must have been a basket. A red basket that could fill three hefty tacos with wax paper underneath. She let me carry the taco basket while she looked to the side, standing and exasperated, leaning on the wall with her hands behind her. She just saw me in the act. Walking down the aisle to a distant horizon yet now I will arrive there soon. I had to keep walking from table to table.

I had to finish the job. I had to find the table. I had to lay down the food on the table. I had to just put the food down to move on. I had to just show my work-ethic. I had to just walk to the next table and ask. I had to get to the end one. I had to just get there. I did not skip all the tables in the middle. I went one by one. I just had to get the table right.

My father was to the left in the kitchen, the tables laid out in rows were to my right. I was in the middle behind a couple of tables in front of the booths. There were twelve booths and a couple of tables including stools by the kitchen counter. I saw the restaurant as a grand place. Small, but affordable. A restaurant in all its senses. But my restaurant. I appreciated the love the restaurant gave my family. I appreciated the way the restaurant ran.

I saw the restaurant with ornaments and adornments. There was a rancher statue, a cowboy with Mexican features, a mustache, and a big sombrero with a holster on his waist reminiscent of (and with facial features like) Yosemite Sam.

A statue of a rancho guy with a blanket over his soldiers. The blanket was a squared-patterned, green and gray fleece blanket with stripes and strings on the ends. The statue of the Pancho Villa-like ranchero guy had a big, giant, golden-yellow hat on his head. His mustache was long with whiskers pointing up at the ends. He had a holster with a revolver in it. A brown revolver. The ranchero guy had blue pants with boots, cowboy boots. Mexican boots. I saw the guy, short-statured, and grimaced over the guy. He was about my height. I had to admit I liked the restaurant with gumball machines by the side of the guy. The statute had a stark resemblance to Emiliano Zapata and Mexican revolutionaries. The bullet vests across his chest, both creating an X across his midsection, covered his blue coat and white undershirt.

Chapter 7: Food Place St. Peter and St. Paul

There is an old Church in Southeast Chicago, South Chicago, named St. Peter and St. Paul Church. The school was shut down years ago, decades before I was born. I remember the school was never opened, but always served as a social service organization building. There were many organizations in the building throughout the decades. Catholic Charities operated a food pantry on the fourth floor when I was five and offered food.

My mom when I was five five went to go ask for food. My mom never got any food the first day we asked. She asked the attendant on the first floor. She asked where the food pantry was located, and the lady in the front desk didn't decide what to do. She told us to leave and we left confused and abused. We went back to my dad's place and stayed for the night. We went back the next day and asked again. We got some food the next day. We were taken up to the fourth floor after talking to another social worker in the office. We filled out paperwork and headed upstairs. The image of us waiting outside to get in and confused afterwards by the circumstances bewilders me. It's an image and memory that I can't withstand, but I need to understand. I really don't understand, but I was in the corner of 91st and Exchange waiting with my mom. I was confused why we were in the middle of the sidewalk. My mom was holding me by her hand. We walked and walked, We walked to the destination. We walked there and had nowhere else to go. We didn't know how to associate the address. We didn't know how to get in and what to do. Afterwards, we stood there unable to reconcile what happened.

My mom had taken me with her to know what to do. She needed support and someone to know what to do. I stayed by her side. I had to be there to offer support and make her feel safe. I recognized that she was in a dire situation. I had to get us out of there if we didn't feel safe. Or, if we weren't safe. I knew we didn't have to be there. I knew we didn't have to be there in the dark. I knew we were in a dark place. I knew we had to get out of there. I knew my mom had to be safe. I knew we were there to just be safe, but our sense of safety was threatened. My mom needed to know why we were there. I knew my mom had to feel safe. I knew that we weren't to be at the address.

The image of us being in the address is not something I understand. The image seems dark, but we had some light once we got inside. Once outdoors we had to be in the dark again. We didn't know where to go. We knew we had to get out of there. I knew my mom had to not be there. I knew there was a way to get out of the address.

I knew my mom was there to protect us and provide us with some sort of security. Food security. I knew she was there out of God's will to provide for us. What were we doing there? I needed to be there for my mom. We were there lost, not being able to feel safe in our own place. It seemed desolate, the place we were in, it seemed strange that we were there not being treated like human beings.

It was a desolate and gray space. We were in our home (our home block, our home neighborhood) not being able to predict what would happen. I needed to be by my mom's side. She needed to be by my side and just hold my hand. No one had mercy on us that day. God had mercy on us. The next day we went back and a man, an African-American man or it might have been a white guy, provided us with food. The food was locked in a room with a lock and key. The food was government-provided (issued) food, like powdered milk and canned pears, and I didn't understand why they just didn't pass out the food to the public, to citizens. I didn't know why they treated the food like a commodity and not a cherished charitable donation. They treated the food like a prize, or gold or jewelry under a treasure chest. I didn't understand why they just did not think of the food as alimentation. Why didn't they just treat the food as something that God provides us to live, and not as a weapon to abuse others by withholding that alimentation and nutrition?

The school was a preschool that offered Head Start, the free preschool program. My mom signed me up for the school once although it was hard to get in. St. Peter and St. Paul had a waiting list. The school is hard to get into since there is our neighborhood school across the street, Philip H. Sheridan School, now Arnold Mireles Academy. There is low-enrollment since it is a Catholic school that requires paid-tuition and is not public as opposed to Mireles Academy across the street.

Chapter 8: Gum Ball Machines

I wondered how we got gumball machines. The gumball machine had a number. I always wondered who got the gumball machine. I always wondered how the money got in there. What devices were used? I wondered if it was rented, delivered, or sold? Who came for the quarters? I wondered who refilled it?

The gumball machines were next to the ranchero guy. The gumball company would come and refill the machine. I once saw the company guy come into the restaurant and refill the machine, and take the quarters. I wondered, what percentage of the quarters drawn were for my dad and what percentage were for the rental company?

I wondered how we got gumball machines. The gumball machine had a number. I always wondered who got the gumball machine. I always wondered how the money got in there. What devices were used? I wondered if it was rented, delivered, or sold? Who came for the quarters? I wondered who refilled it?

The gumball machines were next to the ranchero guy, the Mexican cowboy, reminiscent of Pancho Villa. Or, the protagonist in the Townes Van Zandt song, "Pancho and Lefty."

Chapter 9: Horchata

There were horchata machines in the restaurant which my mom showed my mom how to make. Up to this day she feels pros of the horchata recipe which she said not all people can conquer. "You dad taught me how," she would say when she would make horchata at home.

She liked all the recipes and teachings of the restaurants. She cherished how to fold burritos. Without ripping the tortilla or spilling the fillings. I had to know how to do these things. I know she learned a lot. She knew how to handle herself. I knew she cherished the shrimp cocktail recipe. She knew that it included Clamato tomato juice. Tomatoes, ketchup, avocado, onions, a few, cilantro, lime juice from fresh limes, sometimes green apples. I knew it had optional jalapenos. Write your thoughts. The shrimp cocktail was hard to make given the freshness of the ingredients.

The horchata was a cherished recipe. It was a recipe that my mom treated as a secret. A secret that only a few could know. Horchata for my mom is a heart-warming reminder of the restaurant. But overall, my father. And my childhood with my sister and her in the restaurant. I know her thoughts were on our past when she would stir the horchata, sandy with rice water, in the pitcher seated by the sink.

There were horchata machines in the restaurant which my dad showed my mom how to make. The machines would stir the mixture endlessly. Up to this day she feels proud of the horchata recipe which she said not all people can conquer. "You dad taught me how," she would say when she would make horchata at home.

The horchata was a cherished recipe. It was a recipe that my mom treated as a secret. A secret that only a few could know. Horchata for my mom is a heart-warming reminder of the restaurant. But overall, of my father. And my childhood with my sister and her in the restaurant. I know her thoughts were on our past when she would stir the horchata, sandy with rice water, in the pitcher seated by the sink.

The recipe was not hard to stir. Nevertheless, a recipe that is hard to come by. A recipe that she cherished, but was hard to control. The recipe called for rice flour, condensed milk, evaporated milk, powdered cinnamon, and sugar. She mixed all of this mixture with about three parts water and one part mix.

Chapter 10: Shrimp Cocktail

She liked all the recipes and teachings of the restaurants. She cherished how to fold burritos. Without ripping the tortilla or spilling the fillings. I had to know how to do these things. I know she learned a lot. She knew how to handle herself. I knew she cherished the shrimp cocktail recipe. She knew that it included Clamato tomato juice. Tomatoes, ketchup, avocado, onions, cilantro, lime juice from fresh limes. Years later, during Christmas I had my aunt's shrimp cocktail with diced green apples. I knew it had optional jalapenos. Write your thoughts. The shrimp cocktail was hard to make given the freshness of the ingredients.

Chapter 11: Church

When I was little, about ten, he took me to talk to a priest at Our Lady of Guadalupe Parish. He had office hours. There was something going on at home, something that we needed to talk about. He took me to Our Lady of Guadalupe Church to talk about God.

He prayed and prayed. He once told me of a story of him praying and praying.

Chapter 12: Car/ Station Wagon

He owned a station wagon. A blue-gray station wagon that he bought with his own money for his mom and children, my sister, and me. He surprised my mom.

My mom always asked me if I wanted to see my dad. She would ask me if I wanted my dad to visit us. She would ask me if I wanted to hangout with him on our outings. I would always say yes. I would hang out with him and my sister and my mom. We would hop on the station wagon when he would get to our address. He would ask where we wanted to go. We would go to the park, or to the movies. Or to an outing. We would go to Calumet Park nearby, or to a restaurant. We would go to the museum or to the Lincoln Park Zoo. Once we got lost downtown. My mom walked around downtown after being dropped off by my dad.

We would go to Calumet Park and skip rocks. The rocks would skip two or three times on the surface of the water. in prayer. He would teach me how to skip rocks. We would throw rocks together, and he would skip them far. We would throw them far. He would skip them over waves far off. I would throw them into the lake, Lake Michigan, on the beach and try to skip them. They would sink. (Now when I skip them on the beach in Rogers Park they skip far and beyond what I imagine they can). My dad would skip them to show-off his skill in throwing. He would throw them at the waves and make them skip the waves, through the waves. The waves would crash against the waves. He would throw them off to show his will to go on. He would throw them off to show his strength. He would throw them to show his strength without lack of effort. He would skip them far and my mom would stare at them. I would try to emulate and they would skink down.

Chapter 13: The Boulder/ Sisyphus

My dad once told me a story of a boulder. The boulder was pushed by his dad. My dad had to carry rocks up a hill with his dad, my grandfather. I never met. He told me this story while driving, and he told it to me too many times. They had to roll the rocks and carry the rocks up a hill. They had to carry these rocks on their backs daily. It was the opposite of Sisiphus for they had to carry the rocks up the hill, and the boulders never came back to them. Sisiphus' constant punishment for tempting the heavens was to constantly push the boulder up the hill, and never getting to the top of the hill. Grace

My dad allowed us to imagine the scene that was happening when he was a child. The boulders had to be pushed up to the top of the hill. Unlike Sisiphus who had to carry and roll the rocks, boulders, or stones, back-up the mountain everytime it fell back on him, my dad and his father carried them up the hill to build what they had to build.

Why does it roll back every time you get to the top? Why does he roll back every time he gets to the top?

Sisiphus dies with the rock. He rolls it up for eternity. The struggle is in pushing up the rock and picking it back up. You have to pick it back up after it knocks you down. The boulder might fall once you get to the top, but you have to pick it up once it rolls all the way down. Does the struggle lie in pushing the rock through the mud, or in picking it back up once it falls?

Why does he practice insanity? Because he is not sane. God makes you pick the rock back up when it falls. For eternity.

Why did Sisphus have to carry the boulder up the hill? I think the boulder fell back down because he couldn't carry it due to weight and strain on his body (him). I think he achieved greatness by pushing the boulder up and not down. He let it go after struggling up the whole way up without giving up. Everytime he let it go he picked it up again. He struggled to find his way to the top. But he got there slowly. Why did he let it go? He let it go because of the force of the boulder and rock behind his back. He let it go because of the immense pressure. He let it go to show his force, strength, and might. He let it go because God told him to put it down when he almost reached the top. He let it go to associate the Lord.

According to the Bible in verse 26.27 of Proverbs the Lord tells us

and a stone will come back on the

one who starts it rolling.[1]

What the Bible tells us is that we have to have to start a bit at a time. Or, do we have to get to the top without any weight? Free of charges, plateaus, or any weight bearing us down? We can roll and hope for the best, or do we have to let go of the weight? Why does Sisyphus roll the rock up? What makes him take up the weight to push it up?

He pushes up the rock as punishment for disobeying God. He has to push it up for eternity. Homer in *The Odyssey*, "The Book of the Dead," Part 11, states

Then I witnessed the torture of Sisyphus as he wrestled with a huge rock with both hands. Bracing himself and thrusting with hands and feet he pushed the boulder uphill to the top. But every time, as he was about to send it toppling over the crest, its sheer weight turned it back, and once again towards the plain the pitiless rock rolled down. So once more he had to wrestle with the thing and push it up, while the sweat poured from his limbs and the dust rose high above his head.[2]

What my dad wanted to inscribe in me was a fear of the Lord. He wanted me to understand that there was a way to roll the stone up the hill without failing. I felt that the story of him carrying the stones up the hill was to build something, mainly me. I felt he was telling the story to my mom and me with my sister in the car, the new station wagon to show us that he

---

[1] *The Holy Bible: Containing the Old and New Testament : New Revised Standard Version/Pew Bible*. (1990). Zondervan.

[2] Homer (2003). *The Odyssey* (D. C. H. Rieu & E. V. Rieu, Trans.). Penguin Publishing Group.

could build something of himself and push the rock up. He wanted to instill in us a fear of the Lord. The stones his father wanted him to take up the hill might have been to build something. A structure. A building. A palace to live or work. But my dad's wisdom was something to respect. He didn't understand the wisdom he was instilling in me, but he understood the story he was telling me. He wanted me to understand the way to instill stillness was through latitude. Latitude instills stillness by separating the weak from the strong. The way of the strong is to let go of the rock and go back down and be on solid ground. To instill stillness one had the the way to instill stillness was to walk on solid ground

Sacred Heart of Jesus Have Mercy on Her

In *Metamorphoses,* Ovid describes Sisyphus "pushing or chasing the rock which keeps rolling downwards".[3] The point of pushing the rock is to pick it back up when it falls.

In *The Iliad* Homer states "and here lived Sisyphus, who more than any man loved gain"[4]

Isaiah 54.10

"For the mountains may depart

And the hills be removed"

---

[3] Ovidius Naso, P. (2004). *Metamorphoses* (D. Raeburn, Ed.; D. Raeburn, Trans.). Penguin Publishing Group.
[4] Homer. (2011). *The Iliad* (B. Graziosi & A. Verity, Trans.). OUP Oxford.

Chapter 14: Motion Sickness

I was in danger without prayer. I suffered from motion sickness when I was little. We would get in the station wagon, and I would throw-up in the car, or we would have to stop the car and I would throw-up on the curb.

St. Joseph, thanks for her apartment. St. Joseph, the worker, thanks for her job. God let her keep her job. God bless her.

One time I took a child motion sickness pill to alleviate the symptoms. I was supposed to swallow it, but I couldn't. I threw the orange pill out the window and it came back, and flew through the front of the window into the car. The breeze and draft of the wind carried the pill through the front passenger window. I threw it out the back passenger window while the car was moving and the wind carried it through the front window landing on my mom's lap. My mom picked up the pill and showed it to my dad.

"Look what I found," she said to my dad sitting in the driver's seat next to her.

It got so severe. I had to take the orange pill every time before we got into the truck.

The motion sickness always started after driving for a while. I was always in danger, scared to throw-up. The anxiety of being in the car caused me to throw-up fast.

Chapter 15:Guitar

I had a guitar that my dad gave me. It was an acoustic. It was a medium-built Mexican sunburst. The guitar was a medium-built guitar with a large body and short neck built for a child or beginner guitarist. It was the usual adornments around the open mouth of the body of the guitar. Flowers, and patterns, green, and brown in a circle, surrounded by a single brown circle around the adornments. Rosette as the adornments are called, the circles. The guitar had the usual black boot-shaped item around the mouth of the guitar. The swish looking black item (which sometimes is patterned like tortoise shell or marble tile). The pick-guard.

I hung it up on my bedroom wall over two large, thick, screwdrivers. The wall was painted a light-blue, gray color which held the room together bright. My dad did not buy me a guitar case, so I kept it safe either hanging on the wall or placed flat on the surface of my drawer.

My dad bought it with his own money. My dad taught me how to play. A minor, C major. A minor. C Major. A minor. C Major. My dad had me practice the two chords over and over. Those were the two chords he taught me. I played them instantly. I played them nonstop for days. I played them until my fingers hurt. I played them until I got scabs on my fingers. Years later, I would learn that that was the way you learned to play. A sign that I had muscle memory. I knew how to play well after years of practice. I played those chords and practiced them well. I played them for my dad one day. He told me to show him how accurate my playing was. I played how he taught me. My fingers had to be curved. I showed him in an instant and in a moment of panic. My palms were sweating and my heart was racing. I was nervous to show him how I played.

He told me one day to grab my guitar when he visited and show him the two chords. I played them the best I could. I played them flat, my fingers against the strings and not curved upward. The muscles of my fingers had not gained strength yet. I was not used to playing yet. I would play for my mom without my fingers on the chords. I would play an open chord to sound off harmony. I would play out of tune. I would show my mom my strumming while ironing. She would iron clothes on the floor underneath a bath towel to not dampen the floor. I would lean against the wall with my guitar in my lap and find the rhythm with an open chord.

I learned those first two chords and then gained confidence to play others and keep playing. I'm with Saints. I'm with Saints. I'm with Saints.

My guitar was black when I was older. I was ecstatic to get a twelve-string. I bought a new six-string with my own money when I was a teenager. An electric cheap off-brand Les Paul that was sold cheaply on the internet in an online store. I bought a cheap one--hundred dollar amp as well. I was lifting tables at James H. Bowen HIgh School at the time. I was a sophomore at the time. It was a summer before my junior year. The guitar was bought with my own money from working the whole summer. I would wear white t-shirts and jeans to work. I would lift chairs and desks for the school. I would help the janitors clean the floors by lifting the chairs and desks off the floor for them to clean them. They would clean them with a mechanical floor cleaner. I would see sweat on the forehead of the guys. I would leave them and pair them by hoisting them one on top of the other. I worked the whole summer and saved all my checks. I wanted to buy the guitar from the get-go. It was my responsibility to save and replace the guitar that I broke when I was younger.

I cashed my checks after saving them for a couple of weeks. I saved about six checks that were paid to me biweekly. I ordered my guitar from Musicians's Friend, an online and mail catalog. I ordered what I could afford.

Chapter 16: Goldblatts

There was a store's names YellowBatts in South Chicago when I was growing up. It was in a space that is now used up by a Dunkin Donuts, a Subway, a laundry mat, an insurance office, and a parking lot. A parking lot. Most of our cherished buildings in the inner-city, inner suburban, and outer suburbs (including rural towns) have been replaced by parking lots. Parking lots. Or empty lots. Lots made for parking cars. Not people, or services for people, but empty spaces. Empty spaces for commerce. Empty spaces made for parking and commerce, to park in commerce. The use of a parking lot is to just take up space. A parking lot is a space empty of need. A space made for one need or many. A space made for cars. A space that is needed for parking and nothing else. I have to believe that the need for a parking lot came out of a need to make money, capitalism, a need to consume space. A need to capitalize and monetize space for money. A capitalistic space made to dehumanize. Mostly they're free. But how do they make money? They make money by profiting out of the pockets of the poor. The need to problematize spaces for profit comes out of a need to dehumanize neighbors. The need for private profitable space is nothing but a useless need to prioritize money over people. A need to prostitute a space that is meant to be made for other purposes and monetize it at all costs. A space that could be used as a living space. A need to prostitute a space that is meant for other business that offer some sort of value to the public. A building could be made in that space. A space for a social service agency, a restaurant, a grocery store, a child care center instead it's made into a space for parking. A space could be made or turned into an apartment complex, a home, a living residence, or a low-income housing. Instead, it's made into an empty space arranged for smaller spaces to fit cars, themselves made to dehumanize. I think a space has to be made for humans. A space has to be made for others to use it to serve the common good. A space meant to park cars is not for the common good. Cars themselves dehumanize us by coursing our identity through vehicles. We care not about cars, but people. People with vehicles. When we drive down the road we might see a face, but mostly we associate the car.

I had a feeling that the store was not going to be open for long. I had a feeling that the store was going to be there for a while. I tended to go in there when I had money and was with my mom. It was like a modern-day Target. A much smaller Target, but with the same layout. Yes, I like the atmosphere of the store and the ambiance. It was traumatic to see it go. I wanted to see the store grow. I needed to just see it. I did not want to see it let go. I wanted to see it last. I wanted to see it grow bigger. I wanted to see it be with me. I wanted it to be my store. I wanted to see my mom and me in the store together. I did not want to see the store go bust. I needed to just chill. I needed to just see the store be with me. The store was called YellowBlatt's and it was my store. It was big. It had four floors including the basement. It had a furniture section on the third floor. The store had a basement floor where they offered hardware for home improvement and appliances like washing machines. They also offered lawn mowers in green which I remember vividly. I liked the first floor with clothes for men, women, and children. I liked the second floor in which they offered electronics. I wanted the store to keep growing. I liked being there. They offered school uniforms. My mom would send me there on errands. I wanted to see it last a bit longer. I wanted the store to just be there.

The store closed from financial ruin. It was foreclosure. The store had a closing sale. The store had huge signs, "20% off" the first week. "Closing Soon," "30% off" "Everything must go!" The fourth week it went up, "50% off all items." During the last few weeks it was tragic. The image was dire. The store was desolate. The store was ramshackled and fallen apart. By this time, the "store" was "805 off". But literally everything was free. The store was shoplifted by this point. Nobody did anything to save it. The security that was there I'm sure tried to stop the mass shoplifting and damage.

The store was four stories tall including the basement. The basement had the appliances and hardware section. The first floor had the clothing and everything else. The second floor had baby clothing aligned with the children's section and toys. The third floor involved bedding, comfortables, pillows, and also furniture (couches, lams, and dressers). The store was the biggest store in Commercial Ave. The store also had beauty supplies, and bikes for kids and adults. The store was large, attractive, and expensive. The store had a large hardware, and home improvement section in the basement. I remember vividly the tool sets, and green lawn mowers in addition to sawmills and other appl;iances for yard work and gardens.

The store closed down a couple of years in my teenage years. I remember I would go to the store with my mom's money, or with her and explore the store. I would go in there and buy small clothing items with twenty dollars or less, and come back empty handed or with the item in hand. I must have been twelve or younger. Probably, nine. We would go into the store to explore after eating at McDonald's. I would explore the store by myself, or with my sister, taking the elevator up to the furniture floor on the top floor. My mom would stay on the first floor looking at clothes. I would wander off by myself and guide myself through the store. I would stare at things then go down to my mom and report what I saw or anything new I found in the store.

God bless rent and my phone.

The store was closed down due financial constraints out of our control. The demand for customers was high and the turnaround was low. The store closed soon after we were there.

The building itself was torn down after the store closed. The property or lot was sold to corporate interest. A parking lot was built and a strip of small business was built in its place. The Dunkin Donuts, laundromat, and insurance agent office was built.

The Walgreens, the pharmacy, across the street was also closed down and a Family Dollar, a dollar store, replaced the store. The building itself was not torn down in this case, but simply, the business was replaced. The store seemed out of place. The Walgreens was rebuilt a block up the street on 92nd and Commercial Ave. The whole corporate store was built from the ground up. Including a parking lot.

My mom used to tell me a story of a theater being a the location where the Family Dollar (old Walgreens) is now. A theater! She would keep emphasizing the movie theater. She went in there.

The neighborhood was built by Polish-Americans and immigrants in the early 2oth century. Later Mexican immigrants settled in South CHicago working the Steel Mills that built our side of the city. My church where I was baptized, received my First Communion, and received my confirmation as my Uncle Jose as my Godfather, Immaculate Conception Church, was built by Polish immigrants in 1887. The neighborhood was built in what was once Native American ground. A worshiping place that still stands.

God save my mom may she go up the stairs.

St. Clare bless us. I remember my mom used to take us out to dinner at Mcdonald's. I used to get the vanilla sundae with caramel topping and crushed peanuts. I craved the one dollar sundae. My mom cherished our Sunday dinners. She used to eat Big-Macs, that was her meal, with fries and a Coke. I used to eat the Chicken sandwich, and my sister used to eat the Happy Meal with an orange soda.

My mom took a Big-Mac meal to my Grandfather one time when my Grandmother was away on vacation in Mexico. My Grandfather ate the whole thing on the front porch while we sat.

My Grandfather loved and cherished pizza from our neighborhood pizzeria, Capri's Pizza, a neighborhood establishment since 1968. He told me to pull the slice out of the box. I pulled the cheese from the rest of the pizza and served myself. "Pull!" he said in Spanish. It was really hot. He was the happiest. He was sitting at the end of the table eating happily. He liked his eggs stirred and cooked, scrambled and finished in one piece, not scrambled in the pan, but cooked together like a pancake, and egg-pancake. He then ate his eggs in bite size pieces with white corn-tortillas.Tearing pieces of the eggs with a torn piece of tortillas.

The pizza place closed down after a fire, burned down, and was never rebuilt. It was opened in 1968 and burned down in the end of the 2000's.

Chapter 17:The treehouse

My brother, M, and my dad and his friends built a treehouse on the tree with a wire fence. They placed two-by-fours They used two-by-fours as the floor of the tree house where the branches split. It was big and ample. They also nailed wood planks on the bark of the tree to climb up. They used a chain link fence to wrap around the branches of the tree. The chainlink fence was nailed down to the big branches of the tree. Some parts of the fence roll were stapled with industrial staples to the tree. The tree was big and tall. St. Andrews, let her pray. God was here. God was there. God was near. The tree was used as a meeting place for M. and his friends. St. Francis de Sales bless my writing. Amen. I had to climb up the steps made of wood nailed to the trunk while going up. I was always scared to climb up and down. Going up I just had to look up, and keep looking up to get to the top. If I looked forward or down I would climb back down. The way down was scarifier. I would have to jump out of the last step. I would look down and pause for a second while I decided to jump down. I had to climb up to the first step while going up. The first step was too high for me to climb on. I had to wait to jump until I felt the courage to step. The treehouse was there as a reminder of a social escape space. I always climbed up there by myself. I never climb with my brother. He had a couple of friends who took part in the building. The friends would climb up with him. The tree house lasted one summer. The house slowly disintegrated. The treehouse fell apart from not keeping up with it, not using it as a hiding place, and not taking care of it. or two.

Chapter 18: The Bike

My dad taught me how to ride a bike by pushing the bicycle. He pushed the bike. He used his leverage to push the bike with me on it. We are in the backyard. He pushed me forward. I was in front of the tree and he looked down at God and pushed on. I crashed into the metal door of the building in the back. He took off the wheels to train and had me ride without them. He pushed me so I could hold my ground. My dad kept pushing me to ride. I couldn't ride by myself. I would get up after falling to the ground. I would look at the ground and know I was going to fall. I would reach the back door of the property, the back door of the house in the yard, and crash. I know I had to prevent it. I know I had to use my leverage to steer away. I chase again and again. Looking down I would fall. I looked up and saw the door, the third time, and didn't steer into the door. I steered away from the door, went around the tree and found my dad. I stayed on the bike and braked the bike by stepping on the ground. I turned my bike left, averting disaster and another scab on my knee and went around. I never doubted I would steer the bike. I turned around and saw my mom and the alley behind the tree. I know my dad was going to keep pushing me towards the door. I knew I would have to walk the bike back to him with tears in my eyes and get back on. I had to climb back on and steer the bike away from the door. He pushed and pushed and by the third time I rode my bike. My dad saw me gain strength. My dad saw me train my bike. I didn't have training wheels. My dad took them off that day with a wrench to start his lesson. I rode the small red bike many times with the training wheels, but he told me one day that he was going to take them off. He took them off while I stood in my small stature and watched. He then told me to climb on the bike and pedal. I was scared to pedal. The first time I just kept my feet on the pedals of the bike, but didn't do a rotation.

Chapter 17: Mrs. Roman

When I was in first grade I had a school-grade teacher who taught me well. She was my first grade teacher for the whole year. She was my first-year teacher for my first-grade year. Her name was Mrs. Roman, and she was great. She wore a gray sweater everyday to school draped over her shoulders, but not worned through her arms. Her arms were not through her gray sleeves. Her sleeves were not on her arms.

Her sleeves were not on her arms. Her arms were not on or through her sleeves.

She had me change my pants after an accident.

Chapter 18: The Sign

There was a sign in front of the restaurant. It was surrounded on all edges by lights. It was surrounded by flashbulbs adorning the *Las Brasas* sign. It was beautiful. The sign was in the front of the restaurant hanging from a metal rod attached to the building. The sign was one the first things one saw when approaching the restaurant. It was adorned with the words Las Brasas in white cursive lettering. The sign had a painting of a large flour taco with meat and toppings on it. The sign had a blue-green background.

Years later when the restaurant closed we would drive-by and see the sign disheveled. The sign was still hanging, but with lettering gone. The sign was empty except for the broken, unlighted flash bulbs along the edges. I would walk along Commercial Avenue to and from school to the store with my mom. I would hold my mom by the hand and stare at the sign. My mind was with God. My mom was with God.

Chapter 19: The music box

In the restaurant we had a music box that played records or songs for a quarter or dollar. It had a collection of records that you could play by pressing buttons with arrows to browse. The records were Spanish records. Customers would scroll through the records looking for songs, artists like Selena, Broncos, and other artists. My dad offered the traditional music service to patrons.

The picture

My dad is tired but not fired from my mother. In the picture, I am standing next to him looking to my left while my father is holding my hand. I am wearing a blue shirt and am about three. He is wearing a crisp, clean white apron and is looking straight ahead.

Part III

Chapter 20: The Riots/ George Floyd

I was living West. In East Garfield Park. There was mass looting. The day of the passing away of the faithful departed. I couldn't get to my mom. I had to just get to my mom. I knew I was in danger, but didn;t know what awaited me when I walked outdoors.

I was living in East Garfield Park the summer between my semesters. I was fighting to get financial aid back. I was fighting for my transcript. The school didn't want to review and approve my previous work. I was struggling to see my mother. I was living in the deep West by the Green Line. My mom was far. In the Southeast. I was living in a rented-room in a two-story house owned by Lara. She was kind enough to rent me the room in the three-bedroom, first floor. It was remodeled. She lived on the second floor with her child and husband.

I was looking forward to seeing my mom. I wanted to see her that day since I hadn't seen her in days. My mom warned me no to go out. I didn't know what was going on. I wasn't in tune with the media. I didn't owe a T.V. and the T.V. that was in the room I didn't touch. My phone was used to call my mom only and text my brother and sister. I never browsed the news on my phone or computer. I was dependent on myself and no one else. I thought I was safe traveling to South Chicago. I traveled to South Chicago. I made it to the door and was utterly confused. I walked to my bus stop and noticed the buses weren't running. I walked to the nearest Green Line stop and it was closed, out of service. I stayed on the platform until the CTA worker announced that the trains were not running. I was scared and confused, but wanted (and needed) to get to my mom.

I had to get home. I had to get to the Roosevelt Red Line. I had to get South. I had to just travel Southeast where my landlord's mom and family lived as well (her mom lived in Northwest Indiana). I traveled as far South as 79th. I took a bus going South to an intersection trying to get more East to downtown. On the way I saw looting, mass looting of shoes and merchandise. People were carrying multiple boxes of shoes and looking bewildered, confused, and agonized. They were waiting for someone to tell them what to do.

I could tell there was Mass Confusion on the streets and on the buses. There was confusion. The bus drivers didn't know where to go. The buses were idle in the streets waiting to go to their destination. Stagnant. The bus drivers were calling their supervisors looking for somewhere to go. They couldn't travel one block without getting a directive, or instruction, from their co-workers or supervisors. I got off the bus and witnessed what I saw. (I saw what I believed). I saw no one moving or going in one direction. There was just calm in mass destruction. People were standing waiting for a sign. People were standing looking to go in one direction. People were standing waiting to go home or the store. People were looting to just be looting. People were just confused about what was happening.

There was mass destruction, windows were broken. It seemed people had to sense belonging. People were damaged by the looting and upheaval. I needed to go home. Their restaurants, stores, and establishments were broken into, closed, vandalized. People were waiting for action. People were confused, utterly confused. People were utterly confused. People were just waiting to act. People were just watching the world go by. People were just quick to act, but not respond. People were just doing what they could do to not answer each other's prayers.

I saw a woman just standing with boxes of shoes wondering what to do with the shoes. I kept on staring and staring. I finally got out of the bus and just waited for the bus to go back North. I couldn't catch the other bus taking me East. The bus driver didn't know where to go. I needed to just stay concentrated on what I was doing.

I waited for the bus to take me East, to downtown, to go further South since the trains weren't running. But the bus stalled. I waited and waited. I rode the bus back to my East Garfield station. I called my mom as soon as I made it into the house. I explained to my mom the riots that were happening and the shutdown of the city. I stayed in doors while I heard gunshots after gunshots the whole night.

I was surprised the whole town was shut down. While riding the first bus, I checked my phone. Something was telling me to just check the news, and front page news sites. I checked Yahoo! News, and clicked on the first story I saw. The City was shut down and in turmoil because of the passing away of George Floyd. Headlines ran telling us, "City in turmoil by murder of George Floyd by Police." I saw what was going on in the news. I kept on seeing and reading how the whole city was ramshackled.

I put my phone down realizing that the CTA was shut down, that I wouldn't be able to get to my mom's house on the trains except through the other routes, such as Ashland Ave. which runs North and South through the city. Such routes would be dangerous and unpredictable. I went back home to my room where I knew I would be safe. I knew my only bet was to get into my room to try to figure out what was going on outside in the world. Ironically, I stayed in my room, laid in bed for a while and prayed. I then read a couple of news stories about the uprisings and protests online on my desk using my laptop. I tried to write. I worked on my short story, "Vera and Laredo," about my friend Auggie and Vane and our trip to his new home in Laredo, Texas.

The rest of the day I couldn't eat. I lacked food and had nor preparation. The stores weren't open and they ranshackled, or full of people waiting for food. Going outside to a grocery store would be unsafe, and detrimental to my safety. I knew I had to get food. I knew I had to eat what was in my apartment.

I ate what I could. I ate the apples on top of my drawer. I ate what was in the fridge, OJ, milk, and nuts. I also heated-up a pizza. I couldn't cook. I heated up what I could. For the most part, I stayed in my room starving, or anxious about food. I cooked sporadically, in my apartment, afraid to confront my roommates who had their own room in the apartment, and who were good people. Nevertheless because of my shyness, I acted paranoid towards others although we were on friendly terms when we saw each other. I ate what I could as I called my mom when I came into the apartment to tell her the city had shut down and not to go out. I related to her how much I loved her and how to stay safe. I had to keep working, I missed my mom immensely. I tried to get to her everyday. I tried to get home everyday to see my mom. I tried to see her as much as I could. Bewildered that day, I stayed home and wrote and heard the gunshots around the neighborhood. I called my mom as often as I could. She told me that she had not watched the news and that she had heard of the violence being inflicted on the city. I was confounded and worried about mom and our neighborhood. Specifically our home. I was afraid the looters would get to our home. I asked her if Commercial Ave. was being looted. She told me that she didn't know, but that the news were reporting looting elsewhere. I told her that the looting was probably going to hit town meaning our part of town, southeast. I told her that the looting was going on West, and it would probably hit Southeast. I figured and pictured in my mind commercial Ave. jebing looted in deep light. I told my mom not to go to Commercial Ave. and follow the noise. I told her to stay safe.

The next day it was chaos. The streets were ramshackled. The windows were broken on various businesses. Almost, the whole street was broken windows and burned down buildings. I didn't go out that day, or the next.

When I finally got home the streets were the same in the Southeast as the West. The storefronts down 95th Street were destroyed with windows broken and buildings burned. A whole store, Dollar Tree, was destroyed from top to bottom. An Aldi's, a grocery store, was destroyed. Capitalism was destroyed, the culprit behind our militarized nation-state. Most is the root of all evil. Money was what we destroyed. Nothing else mattered. It made sense to destroy it all except our streets, our public-works, our needed shared, and cherished community entities. We needed streets, lights, but not stores. Our homes were not broken into. Out cars might have been saved, but not our souls. We needed to sever that which caused harm and endangered our health. Crime needed to be abolished. Crimes agaisn't humanity.

I made it through those two days of not going home. I went home eventually after the city calmed down in the summer of 2021. I eventually went home and saw the destruction of the city. The trains were back in action. The whole city had reopened, re-inserted itself into itself, but the image of a war-torn city remained. The City was torn apart by vandalism, and just confusion. Racist confusion, 95th St. on the Southeast Side was torn apart with images similar to those of the Iraq War. The buildings were half torn. The buildings were at a half-diagonal just nit standing. The buildings down Commercial Ave. were just not there, absently destroyed by mankind. In order to try to rebuild ourselves we destroyed ourselves.

St. Josaphat, let me pray with my mom. Amen.

I doubt my mother cares, my anger speaks to me. I doubt that she cares about my well-being, my anger and those intrusive thoughts speak to me. Today, she didn;t give food, emat to Maxi Max, a little kid she babysits and who we have raised sine a baby.

My mom used to tell me stories of when she was a child, abandoned by her mother and father, and left to live with her aunts and Grandfather. She used to tell me how her aunts used to cook meat (with money that her mother would send them) and feed her slat tacos while they ate the freshly cooked meat.

Today, while I was eating pork, Maxi Max came running to me and stood next to me, obviously asking for meat. He leaned in and my mom asked, "What do you need?"

Que quieres?" my mom asked in Spanish.

"Quiere carne," I answered her.

Maxi Max came back to me, and she asked him, "ya te comiste tu dona?" She asked about the long-john donut. I offered him some meat from my plate. I grabbed a spoon and offered him some meat scooped from my plate. He hesitated knowing instinctively that he was doing something wrong in my mom's eyes. He reached, snapped his hand for the plate then reached back.

"A ti no te gusta," she said. "You don't like that." My mom exclaimed, telling and letting Max know that taking meat was wrong.

I finished my taco guiltily, knowing I had done wrong. It took many months to rebuild the city. The city slowly came back to life. The city slowly built a catastrophe itself. The city those few days was aflame. The city rebuilt, renewed, and reconnected itself. It took time but there was light. The day I went back after the George Floyd riots my mom didn't go out. I asked her if she had gone out to see the streets. She said no.

"The streets are destroyed," I said.

I know I've seen the news," she said in Spanish.

"What do you think is going to happen?" I asked.

"I'm not sure. Maybe they'll rebuild the streets," she responded.

"You should see the streets, Commercial. I need you to see the streets," I said.

"Well, Miguel never takes me," she said, meaning my brother.

"He hasn't taken you out to the store, Jewel-Osco?" I asked.

'No, he usually goes by himself."

Oh, well, you should take a walk with me," I said.

"Miky doesn't want me to," she said.

"You should go to the store now," I said.

"Why don't we go see the streets," I said.

'I'm sure I'll go out soon," she said.

I started to believe that she would never leave the house. I told her if she needed any groceries, or meds. I asked her if she needed me to run any errands. She answered in the negative. She kept trying to get out, to just live, leave, to let her emotions out. She should have taken a walk. I tried hard to just be still. I tried hard to just read, to just write, to just read her thoughts. I tried hard to pray with her. I told her we needed to pray. I was surprised she just wanted to stay home.

Those days were hard. The city slowly built itself back. My mom slowly came back to life. I found the city eager to get back to normalcy, calmness, and peace. I kept waiting for more calmness. I ran through the streets knowing that the streets were safe. I knew that light had shined on the City. The buildings were going to be rebuild, renewed, and recovered. The City was safe. All we could do was wait. Just wait. I saw the City as I wanted as I knew it. A safe City. I saw what I believed. I saw a city safer. I didn't believe in thai destruction. I saw the city rebuilt, renewed, and, overall, re-dedicated to newness, light, and safety.

I saw my mom more those days. I saw her more often, and kept her afloat of the buildings that were being rebuilt. I kept telling her of all the progress that the city was making towards renewing the city. It seemed that the City was in a project to live and relive. I kept seeing buildings, previously shattered, ready to be renewed. I saw a spirit in the City ready to give us Light. I saw what could be done if we just tried. I saw my mom ready to move-on.

I saw the city slowly rebuild itself. I kept riding the bus knowing that everything was going to be fine. A couple of days later after the riots there were small riots. Two days later there were small riots in downtown. People's voices needed to be heard. Life needed to be renewed. I saw downtown renewed and again part of itself. There were small skirmishes and riots against police brutality and the needless killing, violence, and shooting of citizens.

I saw myself as part of these protests although I never partook in them. I saw myself on the outside of these riots witnessing their unity. I kept seeing protests on TV and knew that the fight for human rights was not over.

I kept seeing what I knew mattered. I kept seeing people uprising and fighting for their rights. I saw people riding the bus and train in protest wearing all black. I saw myself as part of them. I knew that these killings were morally wrong. I knew the message was clear. I had to just pray. I knew that these killings were happening based on hatred, police angst, and mass distrust of each other. I knew police militarization led to more violence among us, and more killing.

I knew jobs were few. I knew I had to keep donating Plasma which covered some expenses. The donation was for people who needed plasma. I knew the world was going to be better. I got paid a small donation, a small amount, sixty or thirty dollars for my donation. I knew I had to go where I needed to go. I knew I had to see my South. I knew I had to just see my world. I knew I had to just keep on writing. I knew I had to keep seeing my mom and 95th Street. I knew I had to keep seeing the world.

The first Content Test came a few months after the riots. I remember when I took it for the last time I was thinking of my mom. God let me go to Immaculate. The first time I took the Content Test I failed it, but studied for three months straight. I was living on Belmont-Cragin on the Northwest Side around Fullerton and Cicero. The Church, St. Genevieve parish, was right behind the house. I lived in the back of the parking lot of the Church. I lived in an upholstered, carpeted, and heated basement apartment. I lived there alone. The vents attached to the ceiling would leak water when it rained. I lived there alone while I went to school. I was pursuing my Master of Arts in Teaching and finishing my Clinical Student Teaching experience at Mount Carmel High School on the Southeast Side. I would take the bus everyday downtown and then take another bus to the South.

I would visit my mom after Clinicals, and after traveling to the South from my apartment. I would visit her as much as possible, as much as I could, as much as I had to. I would take my studying supplies, and study for half-hour on the dining room table. I would then talk to my mom and eat what I could. I would go as often as I could when I didn't have class or my clinical teaching. I would try to go every day. I kept my promise (praise). I kept my praise with my mom. I kept visiting her. I was excited for the Test. I studied as much as I could. At times, I would pull the end chair and study sitting next to my mom who was sitting in the living room. I would sit directly below the archway that separated the living room and dining room.

I would then pray a rosary with my mom holding my fingers tightly around the beads. My mom prayed with me. I would then take the trek back North always with the test in my hands. I would come back home from the North. I would always call my mom when I would come in. I had a new bathroom. I had a lonely apartment. It was mine, and I knew I was alone, lonely, and desperate to go back South.

I spent about eight months or less in the address on Belmont-Cragin. I was desperate to get out. I was just eager to get out and move South. I was just willing to do anything to move. It was getting unsafe, lonely, and dangerous to live there by myself. I was living there to just have housing. I was in my second semester of grad school and studying to be a teacher, and taking classes online due to the covid-19 virus. (which shut down the physical campus). In addition, churches were also closed. The bars, restaurants, and public spaces were closed. The grocery stores were kept open, and people had to visit outside in line to get in. My church, Immaculate

Conception, was in the South, but when I couldn't get to the church I attended the Northwest Church, St. John Bosco.

I had one call one afternoon I remember vividly with my English Secondary Education professor, Dr. T. I logged-off the class after I didn't feel well. I couldn't stay logged-in after I saw the class not conform to standards by not following the plan set out for the class. We weren't praying with each other, but just staying with each other. We were just logged-on. I logged-off and went to buy food at the local grocery store. I bought food for fajitas (chicken) and tortillas. I went back to the apartment, and heated the chicken strips with tomatoes, onions, bell peppers of different colors (green, red, and yellow) together with jalapenos and ate them with the tortillas on tacos.

I then received an email from my professor asking me if I could log back on. I replied in the negative stating that I could not log back on because I was busy with other work (and other difficult issues). I stated my wi-fi was not functioning. I apologized. I stayed at the address and continued my work on my classes.

I then continued work on my final project for on emy education classes. I worked on my bed (which was just a mattress on the floor with comforting) while the neighbors wondered what I was doing in the apartment. There was this girl, a sweet baby who I named Destiny (since I never talked to her) who would come down and stay in the porch-entryway. The sensor porch lights would turn on and I knew she was there. I could see the light from the front inside window which looked out into the inside steps and porch. I could also hear laughter (I later saw her beautiful face in the library, she was a sexy-baby together with the girl who lived upstairs who I never talked to either). I called my mom that day and stated that I was scared, paranoid, and that people were outside trying to get to my apartment.

The day of the riots, I was immensely confused, desperate to get to my address and understand what was happening in the city.

****

<u>Belmont-Cragin Apartment</u>

(Those people were never with me. I was never by their side, but saw the girls outside. I saw her walk her white, small dog. I remember she had ink or purple (probably blue) streaks in her hair. She lived upstairs with her dad. The second floor hosted a Church which was in the front of the building. A Christian non-denominational Church.)

A couple of months later I was in Garfield Park where the riots happened. I lost my apartment soon afterward. It was a hard summer. I then was homeless for a bit bouncing on-and-off hotels. I lived in what they termed in the twenties (as far as I read) a "kitchenette" which was and is now a hotel without a kitchen, a lunch-space, adn shared-bath although some rooms had bathrooms for a higher price. The hotel is still standing on the West Side on Pulaski Avenue and North Avenue. There was another hotel on the Northwest Side in Lincoln Square, Lincoln Avenue, where I stayed and kept going when I ran away from home.

I then ran to Bakes's (my best friend on the Northwest Side). Before East Garfield Park (the West) before Belmont-Cragin (which I found through a friend, a classmate, whose mom had properties which she rented out and who was my landlord), I lived in The Nest, a dorm, student housing, at NEIU, Northeastern Illinois University.

The Nest was a mess. Before the Nest, I lived in Portage Park in a room in a shared-house. The Nest was student-housing that was free. I had two rooms in the Nest, consecutively. I moved into two rooms during my stay there and called the campus police over bathroom use. I was under intense abuse. I smoked, got caught, and written-up from smelling like hemp. I didn't do much except study, and go to therapy. I tried to see my mom as much as I could.

I lived in the Nest for free because I couldn't afford my rent in Portage Park. My mom offered to pay the rent for me. I went to ask for financial assistance from the school Dean, the

Dean of Students, instead. I was looking for an emergency loan. I was offered emergency student housing instead.

(I needed to study for the Content Test soon).

I went to Queen of Angels Church which was in Lincoln square while living in the Nest and Our Lady of Mercy in Albany Park. I needed to attend prayer and Mass Services to pray for my mom and myself. I also sought therapy services while I was there. I sought my mom . I had to go to therapy to seek my mom through prayer. Mostly, I sought therapy services because I was alone in the North, and needed to go South to see my mom.

I called my mom every day after Church when riding back on the bus to the Nest. Dr. Calry attended me and told me to go home after one of our therapy sessions. She told me straight-up to go home. "Go home, now," she instructed. She told me not to feel sad, and see my mom (and smoke hemp if I wanted to) when I wanted.

When I was in the Nest, I had a deep religious and spiritual experience. I prayed for three days to get out of The Nest and the apartment (the second one I had lived in the dormitory). I kept emailing and asking (in-person) the manager of student housing to move-out and get assigned to a new apartment and bedroom. I kept praying and praying that day. My roommate and I were not getting along. I kept trying to look for my mom. I ran from The Nest, and went to church at St. Ferdinand in Portage Park. I needed to stay calm. I needed to just breathe.

I eventually moved-out after I found he was unwilling to communicate. I told management that I was leaving student housing. After multiple times of asking and multiple meetings (of trying to figure out a way to get to a third room), I finally decided to get out with help of a friend and classmate. He offered me housing in his home while his mom set-up an apartment. I moved into an apartment owned by her in a building in the Belmont-Cragin neighborhood.

I lived in that apartment for less than six-months (about four). I moved out and lived in a hotel for about a week while I looked for another apartment. I then got an apartment in Wrigleyville. Before that, during my time in the hotel, I tried and struggled to find my mom. I reached out to my mom to know what to do, and where to go.

I tried hard to find my mom. I tried hard to just stay productive while I was in the hotel for a week or so. I logged-in to my last class during finals from the hotel. Dr. D. had his last class and I logged-in. I ate Chinese food from a Lincoln Square Chinese restaurant, friend rice and chicken. Thai was my second hotel in a row I lived in after my departure from my apartment. I kept looking for an apartment. I tried to live in the South, but I could not find the South.

(put in Bible verse about wandering for 40 years after leaving land-for those over 20).

I went as far as 87th on the train, but did not take the 87th bus going East. I moved-in out of desperation. I moved-into the Wrigleyville apartment using my savings (from school financial aid).

I moved-out soon after three months. I stayed there while I studied my Spring semester. I would go to the local library to study not far from the apartment on Broadway Ave and Addison. I wudl study for my research Methods class. I lived there while my classes were online. I had another class as well, a Linguistics class. I had to take the class to remediate my grammar. It was part of the program to teach again). The teachers were concerned that I could not teach grammar correctly due to my confidence. I lived there until I felt out of place. I would go to the gym. I would go grocery shopping and have coffee. I would visit my when I could.

St. Francis de Sales bless my writing. Amen.

Chapter 21: Content Test Apartments

The third time I took the Content Test, I failed it again. I did not pass due to my stress levels and inability to give up smoking. I studied as soon as I moved into the new apartment. I was motivated to keep studying the Content Test in my new address. I signed up for a new therapist at school provided by the university, Northeastern Illinois University. I logged-on as soon as I moved into the new apartment. I logged on and told my new therapist Dr. Kneak, that I was alone and that I didn't want to smoke. I told her that I didn't want to be alone in that apartment which was unfurnished, but I had my laptop. I moved-in at the beginning of March. I logged-on from my laptop, and she seemed confused, worried, and astonished that I was alone in my apartment. She didn't seem to understand why I was alone. She was bewildered that I wasn't with my mom. I kept telling her that I felt in danger. I kept telling her that I needed to see my mom, and that I thought my mom was in danger. I kept telling Dr. Kneak that I needed to see the South. I told her that I used to live in hotels. I told her that I got the address fas due to my housing instability. I told her that in the past I was living in hotels, trains, abs other places like shelters. I told her I found a way to be stable in my housing.

I told her that I was looking forward to re-taking the Content test. I told her I needed the address, the apartment, the studio, to study and retake the Content Test. I told her, Dr. Kneak, that I needed therapy to pass the (adequate and appropriate) plan of action the education department at Northeastern Illinois provided to me (the PCP-). I had to get therapy to retake Student Teaching in addition to taking a Linguistics class, re-registering for a class, and asking for a letter-grade change from the department.

I stayed at the address for the remainder of the Spring Semester (it was in the beginning of March when I moved-in). I stayed the whole summer. I took the Content Test at the end of April or beginning of May. I did not pass it (the third time I had taken it). I did not find my mom that morning. I went straight downtown to take the test. I went to an office address on Michigan Avenue. I took it in a room where I had failed the test before. I took it in a chair staring at the screen for about two hours, closer to three. I had a time limit of three hours to finish the test of one-hundred questions. I answered all of them full of anxiety. I kept looking out the window, looking for my mom, praying for her, and looking forward to seeing her after the test. The test itself was hard to get through. The questions weren't what I thought they would be. I found it hard to concentrate for a full three hours. I prepared myself for the test by practicing concentration exercises daily. I did this by taking daily practice tests of all the sections in the test. I took a practice test everyday for a couple of months. I roof the test to pass. I did not pass the test due to a lack of concentration.

I needed to get up to use the bathroom. I came back into the room for a second time, and fell. I did not pass the test due to a lack of practice. Maybe it was a lack of mindfulness, including concentration, understanding, and a lack of clear thinking. I lacked thoughtfulness. I kept trying to get to mom. I tried to pass the test through heart, but I still had to work hard.

Chapter 22: Try three

I didn't pass the test, and due to my lack of confidence from not passing the test, I did not go home South. I went back to my apartment, I was downtown, in Cielo, I just needed to get to Inferno. Instead, I went North to outer space. I lived in the a[artment for a couple of months. I smoked hemp, and saw a prostitute. I walked to the girl's room which was disguised as a massage parlor. I spent too much money. I spent money I didn't have. I walked to Ashland Ave. I didn;t know where to go. I came home on the train and laid in bed wondering how to move forward.

I then grabbed my phone and looked-up the girl. I walked after smoking. I walked briskly, and what seemed to me an immense distance when in reality it was probably three miles. The day was dark, but I had some light.

After the third time, I took a break and didn't study for a bit. I took a break to just decompress. I had to build my strength. I had to build my confidence. I had failed once, twice, and three times. The first time I scored eighteen points lower than needed to pass the test. The second time I scored a couple of points lower than the fist test (it was the lowest score so far). The third time I improved my score and almost passed. I missed it by three points. [5]

I succumbed to a bout of unconfidence a couple of days before the test (this third time). I smoked hemp a couple of days before the test. Three days before the test, I broke down. I was tired of studying. I got overstressed, overwhelmed, and overburdened. I couldn't concentrate. I was burned-out. I didn;t make it to the finish line. I stopped studying close to the end.

Chapter 23: Fourth Content Test

The fourth content test was different. I was in communication with my mom. I took the test after I saw my mom at home. I visited her and had dinner. I went all the way South. I ate

---

[5] (The fourth time, the second time I took the test while living in the Roger's Park apartment, I failed and scored lower than the third time.)

with her, had breakfast with her, and relaxed with her. I then went to my scheduled test at 4 o'
clock. It was at a different location, a different office, a different room. I had a different office
worker checking me in at the counter, giving me a locker key, and telling me to put my stuff
away. She was giving me directions. I scored the highest. I took the test, and thought I would
pass it. I didn't. Before getting to the test center, I walked around.

I spent two-and-a-half years studying to be a teacher only to drop out at the end, not
finishing what I started, and looking to find something new. It's better to end something than to
start something, I read in The Holy Bible. I ended-up going to the hospital after flunking out, and
removing myself from student teaching. I saw my Grandmother a few days after I removed
myself from the program, my Madrina from baptism. She was 89. I sat down with her in my living
room with my mom peeking from the kitchen. She passed away the next January. I bought her a
sweater, but never gave it to her.

On the day of her passing away, I came back to my apartment in the North, and wrote
the following diary entry:

St. Francis de Sales bless my writing. Amen.

Today, 1/6/21

Today, my Grandmother, my Madrina, passed away. She faithfully departed around 3pm.
I was not with my mom although I was in the South. I was with my mom around one. I left and
went downtown.

It's my dream and my Madrina's for me to be a CPS teacher, a teacher or Catholic
teacher. I did not log-on to a group interview today for a CPS Teacher Residency. It was from
9:30am to 11:00am. I received a message around 1pm informing me that I was removed from
the program due to a lack of communication. I read The Bible and found an answer. I need to try
to finish what I started.

God bless my Madrina, my Grandmother. Eternal Rest Grant Unto Her and Let the
Perpetual Light Shine Upon Her.

When Delani was in the hospital she would call her mom and her roommate Elizabeth at Augustana College. Elizabeth will live and graduate from Augustana College and see her mom and dad every weekend. She will let go of Delani, and get her own room off campus. Delani will find her father and live in Moline. God let Elizabeth find a new college. She will graduate from a new college. Delani will stay safe at Augustana College and retire from old age in Moline, IL. Elizabeth will survive.

I saw my Grandmother at the hospital before she passed away.

I visited her at Trinity Hospital three times. I saw her suffer in the hospital. I saw her fro three days, and I didn't understand. I knew she had suffered a hip injury. I knew she had fallen. I knew she was in pain. I knew she had had surgery on her leg. I knew she probably needed a hip replacement. I knew she would probably walk again. I knew she would probably get out of her hospital bed. I knew she would probably be fine if we just talked.

A couple of days later she was taken away and transferred to a nursing home. I never saw her at the nursing home. I never went to drop-off her last gift. I saw her the last day (one of her last days) she was in the hospital. I saw her trying. She waved me off. Although, I was supposed to go back up. I went to see my mom after each visit. I also had an interview before the second visit.

Chapter 24: The Arts School

After my conflict with my coordinating teacher she scheduled a meeting with the assistant principal and my university coordinator. I didn't give myself time to process what was happening. My university supervisor texted me, Dr. C., and left a voicemail informing me that my CT was requesting a meeting, and informing me to not show-up the next day to school (this was

Wednesday) until Friday. I refused to go to the meeting. I informed the university supervisor and my CT that I was removing myself from Student Teaching. I sent an email. It's better to end something than to start something.

I texted fast. I went back to the Northeast Side of Chicago, to Rogers Park, and I read the texts fast. I took action without advice. All I knew was that I wasn't supposed to go into the meeting. According to a dream I had. I knew the meeting was something to not be in full presence with the One we call God.

I skipped the meeting, removed myself, and never went back to the school. I kept the laptop which is not my property. A laptop belonging to CPS. A couple of days later, I got an email (from an office worker requesting for me to pick up my new school ID card). I responded from home on my phone when my Grandma was home. She visited after I removed myself a week later. She was at home. I called my mom that morning and she told me to go home telling me that my Grandmother was at home. I sat next to her on the couch. (Hearing my Grandfather's voice instructing me to sit) I sat calmly.

After she asked me if I was a teacher (something she had been asking me for years after college every time she saw me. It was her usual routine, slightly tortuous), I went into the kitchen. My Grandmother followed my mom. I stood in the kitchen with my phone in my hand which I usually don't do.

That day she told me to text what I needed to pick-up my staff ID. She told me to email the office worker in addition to the assistant principal whom I CC'd. I asked if I could come back to the school. I communicated that I removed myself from the school, and that I canceled a meeting. I did all this while standing in my kitchen with my phone in my hand. I also sent a couple of emails to Catholic Schools requesting information on subbing in the Archdiocese of Chicago. I sent an email requesting interviews.

I never walked back into the school. The school was a former community elementary school turned charter high school. The school was the Arts School in Humboldt Park. I never went back due to conflicts. I got along well with the teachers.

The school is a school geared towards the arts. I stayed until I gave the first lesson. After the first lesson, I thought I would successfully give the second lesson. We had a meeting in the school's auditorium. I got into a brief argument with my Coordinating Teacher (CT), the teacher of the classroom, about my liberty to move around the school building. I told her I didn't like to text back-and-forth and be on my phone. I told her that I was in the place she wanted me to be, the lunchroom. I told her that I had received a previous email about my whereabouts. She had instructed me to stay in the lunchroom and texted me asking me where I was and if I was in the lunchroom. I told her I was walking around the building trying to relax. I told her I was in the library on the third floor, and not in the lunchroom on the first floor. I told her I needed space. I told her, and asked her, and pleaded with her to give me space inside the auditorium. When we were scheduled for a faculty meeting and were standing outside the auditorium doors. I told her that I didn't like us on top of each other. Sometimes I needed breathing room, and needed to step out of her space, tp step out of the classroom, and to step into the hallway, and then come back to her.

I just needed room to breathe. I needed time. I needed space and freedom to move around. I needed to just have liberty and exercise my right to move around. I needed to just be me, and move when I needed to move. I went back home after removing myself from Student Teaching. I went every day. I went to see my mom and no one else. I went to hang out in the South.

I went every day after Church. I went to St. Peter's Church downtown everyday, or to Holy Name. Sometimes, at times, I went to St. Ita, on Sundays. I went to church at Immaculate Conception most Sundays. I was hungry and thirsty and went to go look to quench my thirst and fulfill my hunger. I didn't go back to student teaching. I sent resumes to Catholic school and CPS school looking to teach as a substitute or long-term sub. I was looking for a position that did not require a full teaching license, but could use my substitute license. I sent resumes to school in Evergreen Park, both Catholic and public. They were elementary schools. I felt I was getting a demotion, a thought I could not conquer or understand.

I tried to sub in high school as well, but no one answered. I had gained my sub license a couple of years ago through the usual channels. All I needed was to pay a nominal fee of sixty dollars to gaine my license. The State of Illinois also asked for a Bachelor's degree which I had. The license required was good for six years. I never used my substitute license due to my city debt. I owe the city more than one-thousand dollars due to parking tickets. I owned a Hyundai Accent hatchback, two doors, it resembled a mini-station wagon. I never acquired a city sticker to park in city parking spaces (mostly in our own city streets in our home blacks).

Chapter 25: The Last Test (untaken)

I had one more registered test to take. The test was registered for my birthday around November 12. I had not passed the last one which I took before the last semester started in August (the fourth one). This registered test was the fifth one registered for. I unregistered for the test, but I couldn't get a refund. I canceled it due to my own removal from student teaching. On my birthday, I didn't go to the test center, instead I went home. I went home to see my mom, sister, and nieces and nephews. I bought a cake from one of the local grocery stores. Most importantly, I ate pozole. My mom made it just right. I spent the day with them.

Someone on the train when I was traveling South (while still on the train) reminded me of the test. I could hear their thoughts (or read their thoughts). They blessed the Content Test. I seemed to hear. It was a girl on the red line. I went straight home.

On my birthday, I came back North glad I had seen my mom and eager to move on. I kept on writing and riding. I kept going home. I kept going to my apartment to write. (I kept my room on the top corner of a building like The Bible states. It's better not to move around. I kept reading The Bible. It's better to just stay in one place, one space. I learned a lot by just reading, and staying still. I read what I read and learned to apply. I don't doubt that I have faith. I keep o n seeing what I'm believing. I kept on writing and riding. I think the act of writing prevents me from ignoring my thoughts. Write your thoughts, Mr. Abrams used to instruct us in A.P. English at Chicago Discovery Academy on the James H. Bowen High School campus two blocks away from home.

I went forward and kept going. I kept seeing my mom, and kept on receiving Holy Communion in church which meant that I kept praying. I went to my address as much as I could. I saw my mom struggle to understand why I wanted to teach. I failed to understand what she did not understand about my teaching. I kept telling her where I was, what I was doing, and what kind of teaching I was doing. I told her I was teaching in Humboldt Park. I told her what school I was teaching, and what I was doing. I told her what, where, and when. I did not tell her how or why. The why was _________? I could not understand why. I kept trying to tell my mom I was actually teaching. It seemed she didn't know what to do with the situation, and my struggle to just teach. She had seen me logged-on to my online classes (during COVID) during my first stint in student teaching. I was logged-in to teach.

I kept logging-in during my first stint. I had a tough lesson during my classroom time in my mom's house (sitting on the dining room table with my legs tucked under the brown chair). I kept swinging them back-and-forth. I had a grammar lesson drawn-up. I presented the class my Google Slide presentation. It was crap. I stumbled over the slides. While looking over the slides, I stumbled and could not come through. I kept looking at the video loop and feedback of the classroom on my screen. I kept looking at the camera on the monitor, and my own reflection on the screen. While trying to pronounce my syllables that were read on the screen. I had no faces to interact with or look at. I only had a couple of images on top of their names. I had emoticons to abbreviate my emotions. While staring at my teacher, I did not know what to say. I didn't know COVID was going to take my soul, but God gave me the strength.

Chapter 26: Interviews

I kept struggling to teach. I interviewed at a couple of places. I interviewed at some Catholic schools. I went to the Southeast to interview. I kept trying to write. I kept trying to just keep teaching. "Just" is hyperbole. So, don't use hyperbole. "Just" can mean right, only, or barely. "For the mere act of teaching," is a phrase that kept coming to mind. This is hyperbole.

I was full of guilt over not teaching. I wanted to teach in order to just teach. Most likely, I wanted to teach in Mrs. M's classroom. Most likely, I wanted to go back to my classroom. Most likely, I wanted to go back to my students. I kept trying to find my right placement despite the fact ath I had placement. I kept trying to find my scale despite the fact that I had a space to teach. I kept trying to find my right placement. I kept trying to find my school. I kept trying to find my experiences. I kept trying to just find a way to teach, but I know I was teaching.

I kept trying to readjust and recreate and revise my past teaching experiences. I kept trying to point back to my past schools. I had an interview at a small school named Christ The King on the Southeast Side which is an elementary school. I was interviewing for a long-term substitute position. I ran to the school. I knew that was the place I did not belong. I have taught at the secondary, college and university level. I knew I was in the wrong building. The secretaries kept waiting for me to go. I could not fit in and I could not understand why I was there. I knew I had removed myself from teaching therefore I needed to move on. I had to listen and pray.

When I was in the hospital, I saw my Grandmother in bed, bed-ridden. I kept talking to her about her. She kept asking me where I wanted to live. She kept asking me if I wanted to live in my old room. It seemed (and this is a bad thought) that she was not in touch with reality. It seemed to me that all she wanted to do was live in her own reality. It seemed she kept looking for an answer or explanation. She seemed confused (to me) and did not understand how or why she was in the situation she was in. She kept looking for somewhere else to go. She seemed to know that she needed to think differently. She passed away. Faith was what kept her alive. Faith was what was going to keep her clear. I kept trying to tell her to stay alive for ten more years. I prayed that she would live. She seemed to understand that she was going to pass away soon, but she wanted to let me know she was going to go. She wanted to let me know that she wanted to live and to pray for her to live. She was not saying goodbye. She was saying hi. There was some peace. A few days later she passed away.

Maybe how I last saw her was not how I wanted to see her go. I last saw her sitting in her bed waiting for hygiene. She was waiting for the nursing assistants to bathe her and relieve her. She was waiting to be cleansed. She was waiting to stand-up. She could not stand-up. She seemed to be communicating, "leave me here." She saw me on her room entrance, her doorway, and waved me away. She gestured "wait a bit," putting her index finger and her thumb close together. Wait a bit.

I went down to the chapel to pray. I never went back up.

I went up again the next day. She had already gone. She was stuck in an ambulance driven to a nursing home.

Chapter 27: Picture of Restaurant Sign

The sign of the tacos was hand made by a sign maker or print maker. It was made with a whole border full of lights. The bulbs were all around the border sometimes flashing, but most of the times just on. The sign had black lettering. I saw the sign and knew my dad spent money lettering the sign. I knew she was showing me the picture to be proud of my father. I knew we could talk about my dad, and about the restaurant. She pulled my sleeve, and then showed me the picture. My dad was staring right at the camera with a cristo, claren white apron without stains. I was standing by his side. I must have been three. I looked as if I was had just been crying.

I kept looking at my mom asking, why? Why was she showing me the picture? Why now? I knew she was showing me the picture to start more interesting conversations. I saw my mom's eyes calmer, intuitive, and relaxed. I saw why she had been with my dad. I looked at my dad in the picture, and he was clearly saying and speaking to God, "I'm tired, but I'm not fired from your mother."

I saw that image in his eyes telling me that I was by his side. I also saw an image of my mom being left, being somewhere else, somewhere to the left of us, probably in the kitchen or hiding in the back pretending to do something inconspicuous. I saw my dad wanting to be by my side, but unable to do so, unable to find me, unable to carry me (he once did throwing me up in the air, looking straight-up, his eyes focused on what he was doing, waiting to catch me). I was surprised that he wanted to take advantage and care for this moment before it went away. He was (waiting for me to live) looking for mom, but knowing that he would have me for only a short moment unable to reach for eternity.

I saw the sign of the tacos, tortas, and burritos. I saw the menu sign of all the restaurant had to offer. I kept staring at the photograph to ascertain my dad's voice, hoping to see the light in his eyes. I saw the light, it was there, and he was looking straight ahead. Ahead with his head facing forward, and not looking back. He was looking at what he was doing. I saw him ready for work with his apron on. His apron was pristine and white without stains.

I kept staring at the picture, and my mom, and back at he picture. I kept staring at myself, I kept starring at the background, I kept staring at the features of the restaurant. I ketp staring at the sign. I kept straight tat the box full go records behind my dad and I in the picture. The music box. I saw that it was surrounded, bordered, and encased in glass. The music was run by money put into the machine. The music played and was amplified throughout the restaurant.

I kept on looking at the picture while my mom was talking. I was not looking at her. I looked up a couple of times, figuring out that he was in a state of grace (my dad), and that my mom was (not seeing him) mad at him at the time. I saw my dad nto worried (or, slightly worried about my mom. In the picture, I am staring away to the left looking for her. I saw that my dad was looking for a way to stay. He had his place and was proud of his space. He kept looking for mom and just being with mom, and trying to keep me by his side.

There was nothing going on besides my mind. I kept on just writing. I wanted to just be with my mom. I went that day to grieve. God told me to finish what I had started last year. I kept talking to her. I talked to my Grandma about my mom while sitting by her bed one of the three days I visited her. I talked to her about my dad. She was interested in what I had to say about my dad. I told her, "Ya fallecio," in a peaceful way. Again, when people doubt your intelligence they will ask you to repeat things again as if your voice is betraying you. You can choose to repeat or stay silent.

"Ya falleció," I said.

Maybe she was looking to inflict pain. I doubt that that was the case. I thought of the movement as a moment of prayer. I thought of the moment as a moment to pray for my dad. I am at peace with my dad.

My mom pulled tha picture away. I talked to my mom about my dad and slight anger arose. I'm not sure why she pulled out the picture a couple of days after the passing of my grandmother who had baptized me. I saw the picture with the sign, the tacos behind us, the music box in front of it, with my dad and me in front of the camera.

I was dumbstruck by the animosity. I was surprised I was wearing blue (in the photograph). I was wearing the shirt, and I looked in the picture as if I had just been crying, or trying to find my mom (not necessarily to get away from my dad). This was the beginning of January. I saw the sign of the restaurant. The menu distinct from others. I had seen what it meant. I saw what it ments. It meant I had a life. It meant that I had to just abide by the rules, and understand the past to not repeat it.

I saw my mom not in the picture, but I sensed she was there waiting for me. I saw my dad saying with his eyes that she was okay with my mom. I saw the restaurant in her image. I saw her (not in the picture, but in our souls). I saw two men, my dad and me, looking for her. I was not staring forward, but right. My dad was looking at what he was doing. He was looking up, forward. I was looking for my mom. I was looking for her. I was looking around making sure she was not in danger. I missed her even at that young age of three. I had to look for her.

Chapter 28: Return of texts

I had another opportunity to pass the Content Test (a fifth time). I registered again after the fourth time. I never took the test. I ended up canceling the test. I tried to change the date of the test a couple of times. I did it absentmindedly. I rescheduled it for any day in order to keep the registration. When I realized that I was registered for the test, it was too late to unregister. The date had passed for the test when I looked online. My money was gone.

I returned all the texts (all the study books) after they laid on my desk for a couple of days. I returned to the library all the studying materials. I never thought I would never take the test again. I just kept staring at them on my desk, the studying materials. I kept telling myself that I would return them. Something kept holding me back. I kept stalling the return. I kept ignoring the decision to do anything. I needed to return them to the library. I just needed to pick them up and put them in the return bin. I was always thinking of studying for the Content Test, and studying the materials. I always thought I needed to study for it again for a last time until I passed the test.

It got harder after I removed myself from student teaching. I kept waiting to take it again. I kept on just waiting to study, but after I removed myself, I thought I did not need to study. I was not teaching, but I knew I had to keep the texts. I had to keep them in my address. I kept at them waiting to study, waiting to teach, waiting to read. I wanted to know if I could study for the test and pass it. I wanted to know why, I knew the texts belonged in my address.

I picked them up one day and dropped them off at the Chicago Public Library *buson,* the return boc reminiscent of a giant mailbox outside of Edgewater branch. I knew I needed them. I rescheduled the test a month later for a new program, the alternative licensure program at Dominican University.

I saw the fake massage parlor girl again. She was not submissive. She was dominant (something opposite my personality). The second time it did not go well. I just thought I had to get out of there. I almost got beat up. I saw her take the money, and go into the backroom. I was left alone in the massage parlor room. I was undressed. I heard loud noises. She was highly intoxicated. She came back to the room and told me she needed more money. I had given her one-hundred and twenty.

I heard voices of men talking in the back. They were arguing with her. I need more money, she kept telling to me. I said, that's all I got. I kept saying, I need to leave. She kept saying, I need more money. I did the act. She did it well. Again, she got on top. Agan, she asked for more money at the end. I said I didn't have any more money. I tried to get her off the phone off her hands. She sent texts. She would not let me put my clothes back on. I kept trying to put them back on. I finally put my clothes back on and ask her if I could leave. I knew I had to leave the address. I knew I had be safe. I had to just get out before I got beat up.

I finally got out, and regretted the act. I regretted going back. I missed my safety. I walked back to my apartment, and tried to forget what I've done. I kept on thinking. I needed to save. I needed to be safe. I needed to just be me. I didn't need to be unwell. I didn't need to be at someone else's address with someone else's wife. I needed to just live and breathe. I needed to just take care of myself.

I did not regret loving (although loving had many forms). I didn't regret just being there in company. I didn't regret going to where I was. I do regret hurting myself. I don't regret myself.

Chapter 29: Hard Summer: Apartment, Miami, and Portland

I stayed in the apartment for the next two months. I I stayed and prayed. I stayed until student teaching in the Fall. I kept on just sleeping, taking walks after dinner to Loyola campus, and just eating. I kept cooking, going grocery shopping, and riding my bike South on the roads.

It was a hard summer. This was the summer before my second stint in student teaching before I removed myself, before I told Mrs. M. that I needed space.

I kept being me. I kept surrounding myself with holiness. I kept on teaching. I stayed calm, and just lived, and prayed. I kept calling and visiting my mom.

I kept on just talking. I kept on just looking for people. I kept looking for something to eat. I kept looking forward to the Fall semester. I took a trip to Miami and Portland that summer. I ran away.

I first checked into the Hilton Hotel on Michigan Avenue the day before my flight. I wanted to breathe. I wanted to think. I wanted to sleep. I stayed the night. The night went fine. There was a tablet that the hotel provided in the room. I kept watching television and playing with the tablet.

I kept touching the Samsung tablet. I kept watching television. I then called my mom the next morning. I had the coffee that the room provided in the room. I brewed and brewed. I turned on the coffee machine while I took care of hygiene. I also had another cup downstairs at the Starbucks. I told her I was going to take a trip to Miami and then I was going to leave the hotel for my stuff. I told her the rent was paid. I did what I could to get South. I cried on the sidewalk outside the hotel on Michigan Ave. I did not know what I had done. I understood I had betrayed myself. I tried to backtrack what I had done. I knew I had spoken words to let my mom know I was leaving town. I knew I would stay out of trouble if I just called back. I didn't call back. I hanged-up the phone heart-broken and crushed.

I then stayed calm, got on the train, and left for my apartment in the North. I packed a duffel bag. I carried an envelope with my upcoming rent to the landlord's apartment. He did not open. I tried to fit it under the door to no avail. I then went back to my apartment. I sent a text to the building supervisor saying I was taking a trip and that he could pick up the rent envelope from the kitchen counter. I left the envelope in its place, and then went down. I was scared. I didn't want to leave. I didn't want to stay. I wanted to leave the North. I wanted to see the Holy See. I wanted to live with mom. I wanted to see Chacha. I wanted to see the kids. I acted without being conscious. I was leaving in a Lyft. I wanted to go back up and go South. I stayed in the foyer waiting for my ride. I was conscious of what I was doing. My *conciencia* was telling me to stop and breathe and think of my mom, and not my paranoia. My consciousness was telling me I was doing wrong. My conciencia was telling me I was doing wrong, but I did not know how to stay in the room. I didn't know where to go. My *conciencia* was telling me to just stay still. I couldn't listen to myself. My conscience was telling me to do right. According to a rough translation, conciencia means conscience.

I had a friend in mind that I could find in Miami. My friend Kal from my freshman year at The University of Illinois at Springfield. I called my mom from the car, and arrived at the airport. I lande at Miami International Airport, and took a Lyft to downtown Miami. I had not booked a hotel. I told the cab driver to take me to the hotel of his choice downtown, or the fist hotel he had in mind. I did not stay on the beach, although I walked through the pier.

Miami

I arrived in Miami around 8pm and did not know where to go. I arrived at the airport and looked for my checked bag. I found it in the luggage section. I lifted the bag up by it straps from the luggage belt. The belt kept moving, rotating around. All the passengers seemed lost, desperate for a cause. A cause lost.

I took a car to a hotel, a cheap hotel in downtown Miami. One of those hotels with "Inn" at the end of their name. The logo had a tree. The hotel was full of Latinos from Miami, or Miami Latinos. They were Latinos from Cuban descent and heritage, I resumed. Cuban-Americans who spoke the same two languages as me, but a different dialect. Midwestern-English and Spanglish with Mexican roots are my dialects. Their English was common, and so was their Spanish from a Cuban descent.

The floor was full of Latinos like me, and Miami Latinos. I saw pretty girls with big behinds. I saw couples staying in the hotel for the weekend who were at home in Miami. I did not know where to go. I walked through downtown Miami, after checking into my room, walking the streets looking for a place to be, a pub or a bar. I saw a couple of places I liked. I went into a pizza parlor and bought a slice.

I ate the slice of pizza with a water bottle. The downtown scene was no different than Chicag. I saw familiar places, like Walgreens and 7/11, and local restaurants. Most of all, I saw the homeless. Like in Chicago, the homeless were on the streets looking for a warm place to be, looking for food, and looking for comfort. They were looking for other people to be with like all of us. I saw kids running the streets who clearly had goals in mind: go back home. I walked the same streets it seemed. I walked not knowing where to go, but staying around crowds. I saw a min venue that was jumping. I surrounded the bar a couple of times letting people know I was around so they could get a view.

I eventually went to a 7/11 and bought a water bottle. I did not know where to go, or what to do with my money. I was scared to show my money. I knew I had to use my card to not carry cash. Maybe, the act of carrying cash makes you save more since you know how much you're carrying. Maybe the card makes you waste by not counting.

I eventually made it to the bar. The bar that I had circled many times from afar. I walked into the bar, and saw that it was calm. It was not rowdy or loud, but festive. I ordered my regular drink, a Lil Sumpin' Sumpin', and one of their specialty drinks. I met a bartender from Chicago who lived in Humboldt Park and whose family was from the city. He told me he was in Miami for a couple of years. I was surprised we lived in a small world.

I saw a girl I recognized. She was with a group of friends and had tattoos on her arms. She was happy. She was local. She was beautiful. She had a tight, black long dress cut on the hem exposing her thighs. She knew what to say too.

The girl was a hot girl. I wanted to stay with her, and live. I talked to her, and introduced myself. She was to my right. We were actually praying together. After our conversation, I must have said something with prayer and we both turned away.

I never found Kal. I searched for him for one day. He had graduated from a Florida law school after getting his BA from Springfield and had gained a job in Miami. He was married according to his Facebook page.

The first night there before heading to the bar, I went to the pier downtown. The palm trees were something I knew I had not seen in person before. They were huge with leaves the size of a house. I saw them flow with the wind. The bark of the palm trees reminded me of the skin of a pineapple.

St. Francis de Sales bless my writing. Amen.

I saw the Atlantic Ocean. I wanted to be around water. Water is something we are attracted to. Living in Chicago, Lake Michigan is readily available, you just have to turn.

The Atlantic Ocean was there and I saw the coast. I didn't see the beach since I was in the downtown area. I kept looking for water.

I left the next day for the airport. I bought Chinese food and left for the airport. I spent three days in Miami. I had an overnight stay at the airport since I couldn't secure a flight, or book a seat. I didn't know where to go. I could not make up my mind. It was a spur-of-the-moment activity. I reacted and reacted not knowing what laid ahead and not responding to Godliness. I needed to respond and not react. I stayed at the airport wondering what to do. I saw Chicago flights on the take-off screen, but did not book them. I did want to go home. I wanted to feel safe. I went upstairs to a bar inside a restaurant next to the airport hotel. I sat down and ordered a beer, my usual Lil' Sumpin. I sat there in prayer. I had booked a flight to Portland a couple of minutes before and had called my mom. I had told her I was going to take a religious retreat at a monastery for a week at Mount Angel Abbey. I had not contacted the monastery, but was hopeful I would get admitted for a retreat. I was looking for God and prayer. It just so happened that there was a brewery in the monastery. I prayed for my retreat with every sip, "Saints let me take a retreat this week at a monastery." I then called my mom who I had not called in a week for a long conversation. I was not at peace with her, but I found peace in prayer. I called fast. I was ecstatic, in a state of grace, and utmost peace. I told her I booked the flight to Portland and told her I was going to take a retreat (or, at least try) at a monastery. I told her it was only temporary for a week. I felt alien, but at that time I knew my mother was with me. I wanted peace. She agreed with my decisions and the next day I left for Portland.

Chicago High School for the Arts

I had English II for my teaching class. I had to do a lesson based on the Universal Human Rights Declaration. I had to use Post-Its. It was a group project. I had to come up with questions to span discussion of content, analytical questions and interpretation questions. I had to show the kids how to think. Not what. I prepared the first lesson carefully.

I also had English IV: A.P. Literature and Language. I taught three sections of English II with the teacher of the classroom. Mrs. M. had the same lesson. She drew up the lessons and had me organize and write them. I was still living in Rogers Park, and the school was in Humboldt Park. It was a good long distance. I took the commute South to the school. I was always excited to go to school everyday. I took the Red Line train and a bus on Clark and Division everyday. I took the Division bus all the way to Saul Bellow's way which is a street dedicated to the Chicago writer.

I had to teach the same lesson three times. I enjoyed my classes. I enjoyed my second class of the day. I taught my sophomores and juniors. The English II class was for sophomores.

The second class of English II was a class I enjoyed. There was a girl that was always at her desk. She did her work on her desk, and did not get up until it was all done at the end of class. She was in the dance program in the school, and always wore a pleated skirt and a zippered-hoodie sweater.

I was astonished I was in the classroom. I prayed and prayed everyday to be there. I kept going to the school. I loved the students. I loved seeing them. I loved seeing them safe. I loved the teachers. I loved my professor who was also a teacher at the school. He taught a graduate research class in the education department at Northeastern and was a special education teacher at ChiArts. I felt belonging nto longing. I felt I belonged right away. Another of my classmates from the M.A.T. (Masters of Arts in Teaching) at Northeastern was also teaching there, Alex, who was a part-time teacher. Because of the nature of the school, a charter school, most of the teachers did not have full-time positions, but were contracted for part-time work (this left them open to other work outside schools which did not benefit their careers and growth as teachers). I felt like I needed to be there at all times.

I removed myself from student teaching shortly after my first lesson. My first lesson went great. My students were lively, cheery, and optimistic. They were active learners, good listeners, and passionate about their education. They were also dear friends to one another who showed loyalty and commitment. They eagerly and actively participated in group activities (including a "speed dating" activity we did at the beginning of the semester which Mrs. M. set-up). They spurred the moment with joy and happiness. THey called one another by anem.

I had four classes and numerous students. They were all attached to me in one way or another. They all tried hard to follow along. The school, which was a charter school, took students from all over the city and brought them to the central location in Humboldt Park (revise). The students were taken out of their neighborhood schools, and transported through public transport, rides, and school buses to this new location in a new neighborhood. Some of them lived in Humboldt Park, but most of the neighborhood kids went to their neighborhood school Roberto Clemente High School which was not far off.

This new school, which was a previous elementary school bought out by outside interests from CPs, mostly educational foundations and organizations that don't; have the neighborhood's goals in mind. Mostly, unity. The school ran from nine to five, a large amount of time for a high school, and high school students to stay in one place. Most of the teachers left at three o' clock after an hour meeting at two pm. The part-time teachers who taught art (writing, art, music, and dance) began their classes at three pm and only taught two classes: one from three to four and then another one, the last one, from four to five. This was the school day, a long-one. Regular school subject from nine to three and then art form three to five. This is an immense amount of time for teenage students to be in one place with only one meal during their eight hour day. Their lunch was late in the day at one in the afternoon. They had an option for breakfast before nine, but most of them did not attend breakfast and showed up at nine for their first class. Some walken in after nine for their day. The food was not adequate for their age-growth and intellectual growth.

The students were pulled around all day, five days a week, to fulfill the expectations of the organizations (which are not consistent with their own philosophy). The school is an art school.

Portland

I stayed in Portland for five or six days. I was running. I ran away. I arrived at the motel late after midnight. It was a cheap motel with a courtyard in the middle like a college campus quad. I arrived and alid myself to sleep. I kept looking all around the room making sure I was safe. The next day I did not know what to do or where to go. I ran around the motel trying to figure out where I was and my surroundings. There was a cafe. There was also a sign for The Grotto. I kept telling myself that I would eventually visit The Grotto. The Grotto was beautiful. It has a church, a steeple. It also has a course with all the stations of the cross, a Viacrucis that you can walk through, I bought a rosary for my sister and the kids at the gift shop.

This was the summer before I got placed for the second time in student teaching. The summer before Chicago High School for the Arts. stayed at the hotel and went out everyday to eat. I did know where to go. I would look upp restaurants and then order a Lyft or Uber, a rented car. I went to a dispensary once. THe weed and the batch was okay. The weed burned like burned paper. I also slept with a call girl that came to my motel. A black girl with a big, voluptuous butt. I also went to a strip club and tried to get into a whorehouse.

Chapter 30: Grandma and New Book

In *GoTell it on the Mountain* by James Baldwin compares bruising and sweeping his mother's rug with the story of Sisyphus pushing the rock. He mentions his "life-long task" "whose curse it was to push a boulder up a steep hill." In his version of the story there's a giant "who guarded the hill" who "rolls the boulder down again" once it gets to the top [6].

This image connects to my dad pushing a rock up a cliff with his dad. That's his dad in the rock. He's pushing his dad. My paternal grandfather. My grandfather on my father's side. His dad is the rock. He is pushing his dad up the hill. My dad told me the story of him pushing a rock up a cliff with his dad.

---

[6] Baldwin, James, 1924-1987, *Go Tell it on the Mountain*. New York: Penguin Vintage Books, 2013.

My dad kept looking back in the rearview mirror making sure I understood. He told the story three times to get it right (with my mom and me in the car) on the three different rides and visitations. Don't let go of the rock, or you'll get another rock. What happens when you climb up without it?

Grandma and her socks

My Grandma was 89 when she asked me to take off her socks. She had red painted toe nails. I remember my Grandma. (I would walk in Rogers Park looking for my mom).

My Grandma was bedridden. She had fractured her hip and was in the operation room. Her right leg had a scar up and down the right side of her leg where they operated. She showed me her leg through the opening of her hospital gown.

She said, "Mira," and lifted up her gown. I looked at her scar, smooth skin, and wondered why she was showing me the scar.

St. Francis de Sales bless my writing. Amen.

I saw her again the next day. It was the last time I saw her. She waved me away since they were about to bathe her and take care of her hygiene. The day before she struggled to get out of the chair, the sofa chair in the hospital room, where she was seated. She could not get up and needed to get into her bed. Her fractured hip and right leg were in intense pain. She was out of her bed in order to eat her meal. I came in and saw the mess in the room. There was garbage all around. I saw the garbage strewn about. I picked-up the bag and tied a knot around it and asked the head nurse, a young man younger than I, to throw it away, and I also asked him for a new bag. I asked him how he was going to monitor my Grandma's medication. He said he would soon medicate her. A while later her doctor in charge, Dr. Mark came in and told us his name. He shook my hand and I said my name as I shook him. My name given to me by my mother and named after my Grandfather: Rodrigo Haro. Dr. Mark asked me to ask my grandmother in translation, about her pain level. My Grandmother asked for her pain to be lessened. Mark informed us that pain medication would soon be administered. He is a bld, black, skinny, tall man. He was sincere, eloquent, and tried to take care of my Grandmother in a compassionate way.

My Grandmother was stuck in the couch and I knew she had to get back into bed. The nurse and I tried to get her back into bed. The first time we tried to lift her up she sat back down. He and I tried to raise her up as she stood, but the pain in her leg was too much to handle. We placed her back down and we scooted her back to the bed. With my arms cupped under her armpits, we moved her to the bed. I stepped away and sat back down in my visitor chair.

The next day I saw her. I didn't step into her hospital room. She was sitting in her bed waiting for the nurse to take care of hygiene. I was in the hallway. I had my black, leather jacket on. I made eye contact with her, and asked through my eyes if I could come in. She did not say a word, she only gave me a hand signal to shoo me away like a petal on a small flower. I went down after she made another hand signal with her thumb and index finger bringing them close together, but not touching. Expecting me to understand: wait a bit. I turned left and went to wait downstairs by the flower shop.

There is a small chapel in the first floor of Trinity Hospital on 93rd St, a non-denominational chapel, a capilla, with an altar and a few seats. I went in there to pray in the semi-darkness without the lights on. I sat there for a minute or two meditating and praying. I sat there and asked for eternal peace. I tried to go back up the steps to no avail. I tried hard to just forgive, and go back. I knew there were no other visitors there that day.

I went around the chapel and walked up and down waiting to go back to her floor. I finally sat in internal peace. I knew I was not going to go back up once she told me to go down. I was not going to go up twice.

I left. I did not know what to do to talk to her that day. I felt like a flower plucked from its place, fron, its garden, from its home. I felt like a branch torn off from its plant. I felt like a stem broken off. I felt like a rose stem with thorns and instead of looking at the beauty of the rose, I felt like the world was looking at the thorns and making themselves bleed. I felt like I did not have any root or anything to hold on to. I did not go back upstairs. Soon after she passed away.

She passed away with death on her mind. She kept asking about my dad, Jesus Perea, God rest his soul. He had passed years earlier when I was a teenager. I was by her side with my back to the window listening to her. She kept saying his name. She kept asking about him.

"Ya, fallecio," I told her. He passed away.

"Que?" she asked as if she was not able to hear my thoughts (she was unwilling).

"Ya, fallecio," I told her again knowing that you should never say things twice.

"Oh, tu Papa," she said.

"Si," I finally gave in. My discomfort at the time was not for her mentioning my dad, who I love and forgave. But for unwilling to listen, for asking again if what she heard were words, for asking if my voice was true, for asking me to repeat.

I felt sick. I also felt at peace. I asked myself, is she hearing my thoughts? I can hear your thoughts, she thought. There was silence, deafening silence. But why? Why was she treating herself like a dementia patient (like a deaf mute). And why was she treating me like that as well? As if I could not verbalize my thoughts? As if I could not acknowledge her?

Why was she ignoring reality? And willing adamantly to create something out of the air to create her own reality, and tell us this is not the way the world is? Maybe these thoughts are not in or at peace.

I went home after the last visit, straight home. It was a hard day. It was full of conflict and it seemed everyone in my family was carrying ammunition. It seemed there was confusion about why my Grandmother was in the hospital, and why was choosing to stay in the hospital. No one knew why she was putting herself through pain. The answers were not clear. She did not have them. She was seeking, or she was not seeking. She stopped searching instead she was following other's orders. She was there waiting to act, waiting for us to save her, when she was sure she could save herself [7]. She needed to save herself. She was waiting to get up. She was just waiting to be herself.

I saw her struggle to eat until she devoured her plate. She gorged her food down and then laid her head. She kept waiting to eat. She kept waiting to breathe.

I kept waiting to leave. I kept waiting to see her breathe. I kept waiting to just talk to her outside of the hospital. I kept waiting to understand. I saw her in the light. I saw her with life. I saw her living. I did not understand why she was waiting to pass away. I did not understand why she was choosing to end her life. At eighty-nine, she had a long life, but God should choose when you go and I think we should wait for his call. When the time comes you should pray. She was calling in God to bless her soul. She was calling for her eternal rest. I understood, but I did not understand.

We had to get back together. The day of the chappel, I had to walk back up. I had to forgive her. I had to see her. I had to say Good-Bye, and try to find peace. I had to try to find a way to be with her by her side. I had to try to find a way to be with her.

She baptized me when I was an infant with my Grandfather. I remember seeing the picture of my Grandfather holding me in his arms with my mom behind him on his right, behind his wheelchair, and my Grandmother on his left. They're all looking straight ahead. My Grandfather is proud and happy to be with me, and to have another grandchild. I can tell he is elated to have a grandchild by his name: Rodrigo Haro.

I always saw her in the hospital by herself. I did not go with my relatives. I had my visits with only my Grandmother and me in the room. I wondered why my mom did not see me with

---

[7] Genaro- The child of my sister lost his life because my mother did not bless his life. He lost his life because my mother did not want him to have life. My sister had an bortion a couple of days ago. I know in my heart that my sister wanted to give him life. I told her to give him life. I saw the prenatal pills on top of the fridge. I told her I knew she was pregnant when I saw her face after conceiving. She was three months pregnant, a third of the day, and all my mom did was berate her infront of her and behind her back, chastising her for wanting to give life to another human being. My mom at times seems to have lost her mind. She seems to have gone mad, and does not understand what mad is. (3/28/2021).

her. When I was young, I used to visit to Grandparents with my mom and sister. Sometimes my eldest brother M. would be there too. I visited my Grandparents with my mom when I was young. There was a long walk back to Exchange Avenue (on 88th Street) from Escanaba Ave (on 97th Street), my Grandparents home, about fifteen minutes. We walked and always thought about turning back to get my Grandfather out of the house. We thought he needed a new home. We were proud of their home. We thought we would be unsafe without their presence.

My Grandmother lived for a couple more days, about two weeks after my last visit. She transferred to a nursing home outside Trinity Hospital. She seemed to have found peace after she was in the nursing home. She lived in the nursing home without my presence. I never visited her in the nursing home. I never got the address for my mom. I got the name of the nursing home from the nurses at Trinity Hospital after I ran up and tried to catch my Grandmother while she was in the ambulance being driven to the nursing home, but I never wrote it down. I ran up after my cousin M. told me my other younger cousin L. was in the hospital room saying bye to my Grandmother. I saw M. in the entrance vestibule of the hospital. She informed me that they were going to take her to the nursing home soon. She was ready for transport.

I asked the nurse to repeat the name of the nursing home (once I ran up there and she was in the ambulance and her room was empty). She repeated it twice. I never wrote it down.

I called the hospital again when I was on the Red Line a couple of days later. I was going North to my apartment. I met a girl with green hair on the train. I said hi and sat next to her. She seemed to be compassionate, and knew I had something on my mind. I felt what I felt. She needed me to call the hospital. I called right away. I called the hospital and asked for the nursing home address, and they told me to call again the next day after the department was open.

I never called the next day. I never saw my Grandmother again.

On one of the last days I saw her, I went North and saw a man laying on the street. She had had an accident. Blood was coming out of his head. He was on Broadway. He had passed away. I went to St. Ita parish Mass later that day.

I saw her again at the funeral. I neve rent up to the body. I got a glimpse of her as I strolled through the funeral parlor, but never took a right to go into the funeral room where the casket and body were. I went straight into the coffee room. I said hi to my extended family, the first time I had seen them in a while. I wish we had met under different circumstances. I said hi to my mom and sister, and boter M. and nieces and nephews as well.

My home church deacon was in the service. I saw the rest of my family. I stayed the whole time in the food room. I said hi to my aunts and uncles as well. I did not see my Padrino Jose that day. I stayed for a while. I stayed for a couple of hours. I told my mom that I was staying there for a couple of hours. I did not go there with her. I kept waiting to go into the other room to see the body of my Grandmother. I never did. The next day the Mass was held for her burial. I did not go to those services. I stayed downtown and went to Mass at St. Peter's Church. I could not make it all the way South. I just freaked out. I stayed home a lot.

Chapter 31: After the Funeral

I took the passing away hard. Mostly, I felt anger, anger and not acceptance. I grieved how I wanted and I wanted to run. I was running from pain and all that was connected to pain. It seemed everyone was waiting for me to show that pain, and succumb to it. It seemed those feelings were what people needed to feel, what I needed to feel, and what was deemed appropriate and what was expected of me. (page 33, 2nd section)

I did not go to the funeral. I did not want to go through that pain. I went through my pain through anger. I went through the motions, emotions, and feelings that no one expected me to and others that everyone was going through. I went through anger and am still. I thought the anger would go away, subside, and get knocked out. I thought it would fall away with time.

I felt anger that I was not at peace with myself over my Grandmother's passing. I wanted her to live ten more years. I prayed for ten more years. She left the hospital, Trinity, and went to the nursing home.

My Grandmother's mind was quieter. She was okay and then she left. The same day I was refused an interview for the CPS Residency program. She lost her breath. I could not log on. I went back North after visiting my mom, and talked to her on the phone. She told me she had passed away.

She did not give herself time to relieve whatever pain she felt. She left and then said come.

When I was at home one day after her passing my mom told me how she was granted her permanent resident status. It was during the Ronald Reagan (may he rest in peace) years. He granted amnesty. My mom had to get out of the country and come back in order to be granted leniency. She had to go to Canada or Mexico and come back legally. She took a bus with my Grandmother.

My mom left my sister who was six weeks old with my dad (Rest in Peace) while she took the trip to Juarez with my Grandmother. They spent a day in Juarez in a hotel.

I had a lot of questions in my mind about this trip. Mostly, unanswered questions. Questions about safety, location, and my mom and my sister. Questions. Maybe they were running from my dad (peace be with him).

I interpreted this scene wrong. In my mind, the child was being taken away from the mother to not build closeness. A newborn child has to be with her mother until she is teething. They have to build an attachment. These are my negative thoughts and the questions that arise: Why would someone take a child away from their mother? Why would someone break that bond? Why wouldn't a person want them to build that closeness? A mother has to build a bond with her child. A child has to build an attachment to her mother? Why would my Grandmother take my sister away from my mother?

Juarez is notorious as a violent place for women. What did my mom see there? What did my Grandmother (may she rest in peace) put her through? What was my Grandmother thinking about my six-week old sister? I'm sure she thought she was running away from my dad (God rest his soul).

My mother told me this one day after I got home from work while sitting on mher kitchen table. She told me these stories while I was recovering from a long shift at the sugar factory/plant.

I let go of my Grandmother when I did not visit her. I bought her a beige-colored embroidered sweater for Christmas. I never gave it to her. I tried to pack it for her. I tried to find the nursing home address. I could never find out when my mother was visiting her, so I could go with her. I only find out after the fact. She never allowed me to go with her to visit my Grandmother.

I could never find peace of mind. My mind was always convoluted, always rushing, always loud, and always out of place.

I wandered the streets one Sunday looking for my mom, looking for the South, looking for my Grandmother. I wandered on the trains, turned back, and called the address, my address and my mom (the mom I grew-up with, the house where I grew-up with, my home). I wandered through downtown waiting for a call, and waiting to see my Grandmother once again.

That day they were all South visiting my Grandmother at the nursing home. I had to go with her. I had to see her to pray with her and tell her to get out of the nursing home. I had to tell her to live. I had to tell her to live ten more years. I had to tell her to wait and to live to see me become a CPS teacher.

I got South and then turned back. It was after the sundown. I went straight left after leaving the 87th Red Line train station. Instead of turning right, I turned left and went into a liquor store. My nerves were getting the best of me. I called home from the liquor store. My mom didn't answer. It was a day of festivities. It was New Year's Eve. December 31, 2021. I could hear my Grandmother's thoughts calling me from the store. I could feel my Grandmother calling me to her. I could feel her telling me it was going to be alright if I just prayed.

I went back downtown. After waiting for the bus, I did not get on the 87 going east. I got back on the train going North. I had taken Communion earlier at St. Peter's Church. I couldn't get on the 87 bus.

I was in the process of getting back to Chicago Public Schools. I had things planned. I was excited, but apprehensive about the program and its application process.

I never saw my Grandmother again. I never told her I was planning on going back to CPS. I never allowed myself to see her again the incident when I got kicked out by her hand gesture (which I initially thought was her kicking me out and which I thought meant "don't come back," but which meant "wait a bit") I never went back up. I never forgave myself.

I went back the next day, the last day she was being transferred from the hospital to the nursing home. I saw my first cousin, Cadena, in the hospital entrance waiting for her ride from her dad. Our other cousin, Beatriz, daughter of our Aunt Rose, was visiting her as well.

"Beatriz is up," she said.

"Oh, okay. Is he coming straight down?" I asked.

"I will text her to let her know you're here," she said. She hugged me and I went in.

I never went up. I went to the cafeteria to brew a tea. I drank it in the lobby. I sipped slowly praying for her, "God bless my Madrian, let me see her," with every sip. I never went back up. Because of COVID-19 restrictions, I could not go up until she came back down. No more than one person could visit her. Finally I got tired of waiting, I went up after an hour. I never found her. She was transferred a couple of minutes before I went up.

"She got in the ambulance thirty minutes ago," the head nurse of the floor incharge of her case told me.

I went to her room and it was empty. The bed was empty.

"Which hospital did she get transferred to?" I asked honestly looking for guidance and direction.

"She got transferred to _______," she said. The name did not stick. It did not ring a bell. In my panic and anxiety I stayed calm and knew my next move, but my memory was not working with me. The name of the nursing home I did not write down. She was riding on the ambulance while I was traveling to my mom's.

The afternoon she passed away, I spent the evening and morning in my apartment and visiting my mom. I opened up The Bible after getting a call from mymom informing me that my Grandmother had passed away. I hanged up and read. I read a section of how people will start to fulfill their promise. I read how those that do not understand you will betray you. I had to show them my necessities. I had to tell the coordinator of the residency educator program that I did not have the necessary tools, my laptop with a camera, to log-on. I read that I would be granted what I needed to succeed and that Ihad to communicate what I had and lacked. Those that lacked will need, and those that need will receive. I did not have what I needed.

I did not know how to get back to CPS. I explained to her, a young woman named Dack who I had met online during a preliminary meeting that I was not able to log-on to the second interview. I also indicated that I needed to reschedule asap.

The next day she emailed me telling me I could not interview. That was the same day my Grandmother passed away. My mom told me that she lost her breath with my cousin Blanca, the oldest grandchild, by her side. She laid down and said bye.

A couple of weeks later I got a job in labor.

A couple of weeks after the funeral service, I applied to a new teaching program.

I always thought my sister should have talked to my Grandmother in the hospital before passing away. It was coincidental that my Grandmother was 89 at the time of passing and my sister was born in '89.

I applied to St. Xavier University. They have an alternative licensure program. All the program required is a small part-time internship followed by a full-time teaching gig. The program also allows you to get a Master's which leads to a 9 (full-time teaching license).

I got in late into another alternative teaching program at Dominican University.

I bought work boots the day the program called me to inform me of their decision and interest.

I was in Walmart browsing on 83rd and Stewart. I was informed that I could apply to the program without my latest transcripts which I was told I could not get out. I was told to apply without them. I was in what I considered my land. I guess I did not have enough money. I guess my education cost money.

I had been reading The Bible and came upon passages about keeping your land, the land where you live, and the land that your ancestors gave you. I learned you can't keep you land until after frosty years of wandering. This is in case you leave before you turn twenty. All those under twenty who wander will wander for forty years. Unless you come back and bear arms. I had also been reading about how to get back your land.

The Holy Bible mentions that you have to take all your fruit from your current dwelling and place them in a fruit basket for you to take to your land. You have to take that offering to the place of your choosing. Your palace of prayer. You also have to take votives wrapped in a loincloth. I did all this.

The Bible also states that after you take your offerings you have to pray in the address for eight days. A person seeking to claim back his or her land has to pray in place and then on the eight day they can come out. The loincloth was my blue winter coat which my mom told me to buy.

The Bible also states that the person seeking to come back to Land has to pour grout and rocks on the building. Thai was something foretold in The Bible. I have not yet poured grout and rocks on my address.

I offered, and kept offering, votives and fruits to my address on Exchange Ave. where I grew up ever since I left Roger's Park and thereafter.

I applied to Dominican University soon afterwards. I kept looking for programs. I applied after being rejected by St. Xavier University which is in the far South. I tried hard to get my applications together. I tried hard to just have an application. I tried to apply as fast as possible. I got rejected by the second school which was St. Xavier University. I also applied to The University of Illinois at Chicago, which was my first application. I applied to a Creative Writing program to gain an M.A. I awaited the decision from UIC while I applied to St. Xavier. I had to complete my application to St. Xavier, but did not get my graduate transcripts from NEIU released. I applied to Dominican University with a Fall application. I did not get my transcripts released from Northeastern Illinois University (NEIU), but notified them of my grades not being available. I did not get back to school to release my transcripts. I told the university, Dominican, I could not provide my transcripts. I notified them I had teaching experience. I sent resumes with my experience. I kept looking for the right school.

I did not pass the Content Test. I looked up schools on the Illinois State Board of Education (ISBE-pronounced eesbee) website. I looked for alternative programs that required higher standards, a shorter apprenticeship program (an internship, a residency, a short stint before gaining teaching credentials.

I then applied, looked up the programs close to me, close to Chicago. I applied to the schools that would accept a B.A. and schools that had a teaching program in English Language Arts (ELA0. I saw that all the programs required the Content Test as well that I did not pass.

Around this time I applied to labor agencies as well. I read in the Holy Bible that those that had not finished what they had started the year before should not do something new. They required to work in labor for an unspecified amount of time to get back to what they had started (which I presumed was forty days). The new year brought new things, especially wisdom. I learned that I had to get back to teaching and I was not going to do that through drinking milk.

I read in The Bible as well that those that did not learn to be teachers would drink milk like children to learn right from wrong. They would be weaned off solid food until they learned to not do wrong. The new year provided an opportunity to finish what I had started last year.

I kept reading The bible. I kept looking for labor. I kept looking for a way to leave milk. I finally did. I stopped putting milk in my coffee. I learned to just breathe. Around this time, I also broke my ribs.

I slipped and broke my ribs in front of the Church on my walk home. It happened in the alley. I slipped and damaged my right side and the ribs. I went home bruised and without breath. I could not breathe properly because of the damaged ribs. The ribs did nto allow my lungs to fill up completely, so I had to take deep breaths to exercise my lungs. The pain went away as the lungs got stronger.

My lungs were damaged. My ribs were broken. I felt out of breath. On the day of the funeral, I could barely stand. I did not sit there in immense pain while I breathed. Mostly, I breathed. I have to keep on breathing, I thought. I took deep breaths to fill my lungs. When I went to the hospital, the doctors and nurses told me to take deep breaths to fill up my lungs. I could cause damage which could lead to a lung infection caused by shortness of breath, and the inability to open up my airways. Some of the symptoms I had like coughing and wheezing were a product of my damaged lungs.

I went back to my mom after my short stay at the hospital. I kept breathing. I kept taking deep breaths. I breathed and breathed. The hospital gave me a breathing apparatus to fill up my lungs with air. I always got anxious, nervous, and scared that my lungs couel collapse or pop, but that never happened.

I kept breathing and breathing. I tried to fix my lungs only to damage them again shortly after. I damaged my lungs again while working. I found a job in labor to get back to teaching. I knew labor would get me back to teaching. I would teach after labor. I kept working the labor job.

I got a job in a sugar factory. I processed sugar of all kings in the factory. The plant is on the Southeast Side of Chicago close to Exchange. Ave. It's on 10th and Cottage Grove. We melted down the sugar that arrived in pallets. The bags weighted one-to-two tons. We cut these open with box cutters or blades and dumped them on huge tanks to melt them down. The syrup was then loaded up to new tanks attached to trailers and driven to major companies that used the sugar like kellog and Miller.

We moved these pallets around with forklifts.

I tried to just be me. I tried to find myself (when everyone told me to be the person they wanted me to be). I tried to be me when everyone told me to be someone else. Them. They told me to be them without any (reluctance) remorse, or without any care. They did not care who I wanted to be. The "they" is up to interpretation, maybe I just needed someone to blame for my own personal and career failings. I wanted to be me in the Southeast and be the best I could. I guess my identity is made up of different concurrent parts. I like the Southeast me. I like me when I am Southeast, but "they" wanted me out. I needed to move West soon. My Grandmother never believed in me, in my writing, or in my reading (Lord forgive me). She never wanted me to read anything else besides CPS studd.

One day during a visit I stared at a book I had left it on the dining room table and I could tell she did not want me to read it. We both stared at it as if it was a foreign object. I eventually finished the book. There was another time when my Grandmother, together with my mom, did not let me into the address (it was for her birthday). My Grandmother was sleeping on my mom's bed and I was left out on the porch. I waited for her to open the door. I kept waiting for her to just be with me. I guess I did not listen.

I guess I just had to teach. I just had to do it.

One day while on the train, I saw a couple. I was thinking of Sisyphus. The landlord of a Pilsen building had recently asked for a credit report which I did not have, but could provide. I was hard on myself and required it to approve my apartment. He was adamant that he receive it, and would not even consider talking about anything else, even rent or a deposit. I mentioned the credit report, and that I felt that we were like Sysiphus pushing the rock up the cliff. "Empujando la roca," he mentioned.

I basically was hinting that we were not seeing eye to eye. I mentioned that maybe we should let go of the rock. Or better yet, (to understand the fable better) to keep pushing it until it falls back down again. I also saw a passenger on the bus and I asked her if she needed help carrying her extra duffel bag. She said no. She stared at me halfway up the train station steps while carrying her up, pushing her own rock up the cliff, and then started right at me when she got to the top, stepped on the train and sat while staring at me.

The couple was a close couple, and I thought about them, and ten wrote this note:

Sometimes, at times, we stand on the rock instead of pushing it forward, as if we're taller than the rock, standing clear of ghosts, looking over the horizon at the cliff, knowing we'll never get on top, knowing we'll fall back down if we don't push it up. Standing taller than the rock as if it were unmovable. The rock can't be pushed if you're standing on it.

While reading Richard II by William Shakespeare I came upon a scene in Act I, Scene 3, lines 60-561, that relates to Sysiphus, an allegory of a father pushing the rock for his son and his father as well. Gaunt speaking for Bolingbroke, his son, says:

God in thy good cause make thee prosperous

Be swift like lighting in the execution

Ane let thy blows, doubly redoubled.

(they are both pushing the rock trying to usurp Richard II, but Blingbroke is the one pushing the rock for his father, maybe his father is the rock and the throne is the the top of the cliff, later to fall back down.) They are both reaching for the sky. Gaunt, his father, is urging Bolingbroke, later Henry IV, to push his rock and steal the throne. But to what end? What happens when it falls back down? Do we pick it back up, or let it fall back down, and pick it up once more?

My dad had an address, his restaurant, on Commercial Avenue that is now an empty lot. It holds half a chimney, a fireplace in the middle of the property. It is now empty. The building was torn down. My mother used to always tell him to burn it down for the insurance money. My dad never did, and the building eventually was vacated. Years later I would see people come in and out of the address. I wondered who they were.

The building was eventually torn down while my dad lived in another address and we would all be silent. He, my mom, and me would all be silent, staring out the window at the property. I would stare at my mom and dad sitting on the front seats of the station wagon waiting for them to speak, to say something. But they never said anything. They stared straight ahead as if the address never existed, as if it did not exist and as if it was invisible. "See what you believe. Become what you receive." They did not believe in the address therefore they did not see it.

Sunday, February 28, 2022 (October 10,   ). This is the day I wrote all of this. While reading the Holy Bible, Ezekiel 24. I have to write what I feel and I feel fine. I came home on that day after my mom's birthday. A voice told me, "You already lost her." Maybe my own self-consciousness was making me feel guilt and remorse. Maybe I associated St. Josaphat, my patron saint of my birthday. I felt strong with prayer. But also something told me I had lost her due to my own inability to act. I got on the bus and did not walk home due to anxiety and panic attacks. I got on the bus and rode around town looking to go back South, but ended up North. I came home after her birthday that day without seeing her. I was not able to find her or see her, all the blame I place on self. I was staring at my phone, at the things on my desk at the right. A voice told me, "Go back," but I did not listen to myself. I did not listen. I just went along and cooked my dinner in silence and solitude. That day was painful. I did not understand why I lost her, or how I lost her. I didn't understand.

I kept on working with her. I kept on calling and calling her. I kept on being me. I kept on thinking that I would see her soon without realizing that I was actually losing her by not visiting. I realized that there was someone else I needed to take seriously and that someone was me. I needed to take care of myself through her. I needed to pray. I needed to stay. I needed to call, to talk, and to believe. I needed to stay calm and with her, and pick her up emotionally. I kept trying to get there, the stres, noise, anxiety, anti-social behavior and constant turnarounds on the train were a stress. I kept looking for my mom. I kept fighting. I was in a struggle to save her life. I kept looking up at the sky looking to pray.

According to me, my vision of me studying is either to be a teacher or a professor. Since I was little I wanted to be a teacher. I had a vision of me living on the Southeast Side, in South Chicago, one of the 77, and teaching at James H. Bowen High School, my neighborhood school and alma mater. I kept coming back to this vision of me teaching with my mom, of me walking back from Bowen a block or two, and reaching my mom. What does this image mean?

I'm going to pass the Content Test. I have to say the image of me walking to and from Bowen and home is an image of God. I have to say that if the image comes true it would be the second time that I attend Bwoen. I kept on trying to reach that image. Throughout school, undergrad, and graduate school I held the image steady. I kept trying to teach. I kept trying to reach the top of the summit. It's like a rock. I have to keep pushing up like Sysiphus. I have to teach for better or worse. I know too that that is my calling.

I have to just be me. I have to just keep on teaching in the South. There is no other way or story. I have to keep going where the story is going. I have to keep going home. I have to keep that image of me being with Christ and being with my mom (getting along with her).

The Content Test is another rock, another Sysiphus story to metaphor. It's almost done. I can't let it go. I have to osuh it forward. I have to just be me, and go forward, upwards and onwards. I have to teach English anyway I can. I have to be storing by being me. I have to be me with my mom and be her son.

Later in the year after signing up for labor at the staffing company, I applied to Dominican University. I got conditionally accepted. I prayed for forty days (I actually did not show up for the thirty-eight day). I had to make it to forty. I don't know what happened. I spent forty days at the factory. The past sentence is a lie. I walked away on my thirty-eighth day. It was a Saturday. Monday would have been my fortieth day.

I have to take the Content Test for the new program.

I am currently on the thirty-eighth day waiting to get to forty. I tried to stay on Land, my land, Southeast Chicago, on the thirty-eighth day. I had to stay in Land, but my mom kicked me out for two straight days.

I tried to explain to her that I loved her. I tried to explain that I had to take the Content Test. I tried to explain that I was a teacher. I tried to explain that I could teach. I tried to come up with excuses to not study. I knew I had to study. I am going to study.

I knew Ihad to stay put, stay still, and not move until I knew where to move. There was something in me that told me I needed to move fast. I needed to move out of Rogers Park, out of the North, and go more South. I have to just write. The almost forty days were rough, full of disconnection from prayer, full of moments of non-action followed moments of hard labor. I had to stay put. I didn't have enough to eat. I had to just be me. I had to keep working. I had to get on my feet, work, and pray. I had to empty bags of sugar into tanks to melt for them to get loaded in the trucks. I had to move, and stay still, nad stand, and pray.

I lasted thirty-nine days. One more day. I went back to work. I kept on being me. It was thirty-nine of hard labor. I went back for a full shift. I lasted the whole day, ten hours. I never doubted my ability to persevere. I went ahead and clocked-in, ad clocked-out. I also logged-on to a meeting with my new adviser from Dominican University. I saw my commitment, I tried to show my commitment, and determination to be there. I kept trying to prove myself. I kept going to Mass. I kept praying. I kept trying to be me. I kept prayign for my dad. I heard his words of Wisdom. I know his soul is in Heaven resting in peace. I tried to control myself.

The meeting with my adviser went well. It was a study/tutoring session for the Content Test. I saw myself grow. I saw how to study. I connected teaching elements, concepts, and strategies to my studies. I realized with patience I could breathe.

I kept studying. I went home that day after work only to get kicked out again. I saw my mom. This time she did not leave me on the porch. This time she opened the door, but stood in front of the door.

She opened the door and I asked, "What's wrong?"

She looked ahead.

I then asked, "What now?" in plain english.

She responded, "Que?"

I could not repeat. I could not translate (in Sonsich) in order to not say things twice.

I stood there. I stood my ground. I let myself inside through the door. I saw the kids. I saw my Goddaughter, Jazzlyn. I saw plenty of love. I saw God in her eyes.

After the forty of labor, I went back home and told the world I had entered a teacher program again. I signed-up for The Content Test again. I signed-up with the money I had made from work, my salary, I told my mom. I explained to her I needed to pass the Test as soon as possible. I then explained to her I needed to persevere in the face of obstacles, and needed to become a teacher with her support. I told her I could be triumphant with her by my side.

While I was explaining this to her, I was cutting open a mango. The mango was huge, yet over mature, brown and gray on the inside. You cut it in pieces, the sides first. I ate it and then placed the pieces in a row. I used the mango to explain to mom how I needed to put the pieces together in order to teach. I then move them around the plate to signify my success. I took a long swig of my wine bottle.

"I can't explain the metaphor, the symbol. I can't explain it, but if the mango is fresh, I can eat it," I said.

I tried to tell mom how I could teach. I tried to explain how I could stay in a classroom supported by her grace. I tried to explain to her that I could survive in a classroom if I was clear with her about my motives, aspirations, and dreams. I needed to get my attitude correct in order for her to be sincere and in order for her to understand my objectives and plans behind teaching. I offered an explanation from the two times I was removed from student teaching. I was put by the wayside, I explained. I had a shorter path to teaching, and did not see the goal in front of me for lack of awareness. I chose to stray, and to come back to teaching.

I no longer considered myself a student teacher, but, outgrown from student teaching, considered myself a teacher with a full identity. I looked and looked. I found my new school, Dominican, through prayer. I decided to go back to work, and to go back to school. I decided to serve my penance in CPS, and work where I needed to work. I did my forty days, missed two days, and was four days late. I explained to my mom that the work address was not that hard to be in. I enjoyed my time there.

There was a girl named Aris who worked in the office. She was always there when I clocked-out. I always stopped at the window, which was by her punch clock, to say bye. There was a partition separating the hallway from the main office. The partition had a sign, Drivers Do Not Enter Office," attached to the window. The drivers had to give their documents through a hole in the window. Aris's desk was right in front of the partition glass-window. The drivers almost never went into the office.

Later during my time in the factory, Aris stopped being at her desk when I clocked out. She would not be there to meet and say good-bye. I would tap and wave. I waved to say goodbye with my hand, and not my voice mumbling, "bye." When she was gone, I felt strange not saying goodbye to her and usually had a rough trip home full of anger and resentment. I would not get home with her blessing.

I neer doubted my ability to stay strong, but I did doubt my indentations with the girl (and her intentions as well). I was on a path to self-discovery. I needed her by my side. We spent St. Valentine's Day together. I told her I loved her in my mind. Our thoughts were fine. We both had the same sentiment. We both knew we would leave each other's side soon.

I struggled to find my place. I found my place at Dominican. I only got to Dominican through Exchange Ave. I was ecstatic, but nevertheless bewildered to continue my studies and be a teacher again. I got the acceptance letter in the mail. I was surprised to read the acceptance letter. I was surprised by the hello letter. I was surprised to see myself at a university again. I was surprised to see myself breathe. I was surprised that my mom was by my side. I was surprised that I was there by her side. I was surprised that I was alive and well and could pray to the Lord. I was surprised that I was the one. I was surprised that I was me and no one else. I was surprised that I was up. I was surprised that I could write.

I was surprised that I could just breathe. I was surprised that I could think clearly. I was surprised I could talk clearly. I was surprised I could get in motion. I was surprised I could live. I could read, write, play music, and breathe. I was surprised I could play my guitar. I was surprised I could trust in God. I was surprised I could trust in myself and my own abilities and talents. I was surprised I was by my side (meaning I was self-aware) and could be by my mom's side and my nieces and nephews. I was surprised to write. I was surprised to just read, travel, write, listen, cook, and view, sense, taste, touch, semll, look, hear, and walk. I was surprised to know I am with the Lord. I was surprised I had an idea to keep writing. I was surprised I had an idea to keep a writing journal.

I tried to keep a writing journal of all my writing. My reading schedule was for pleasure, but then I felt obligated to read. I started reading E.L. Doctorow and his novel *City of God*. It was the second novel by him that I read. The first was *Billybathgate*.

I found the book in the secondhand store on Broadway, Green Element. The book was not my first choice. I grabbed it after I wandered through a couple of shelves on the bookcases cornered in the store. I had a couple of books in my hand. I put them down to search for another one, a book I could trust, a book I could get through. I picked up the book that I thought was the best choice. Doctorow seemed familiar. I of course had no idea what the book was about. It turned out o be a novel about an Episcopal Church with flashbacks of the Holocaust. I did not read the whole book the first time around. I was accepted, then put it down and read *Richard II* by William Shakespeare. I did not skip a page at first. I wanted to read something else, esp[ecailly since I had planned on reading *Richard II*, I had ordered it from Amazon, and had done some preliminary reading. I had no option, but to stay loyal to the page, and to Doctorow who had given me a first book to read. I went through a groove of not reading although I was confident I would write again. I never wanted to skip my writing schedule.

I kept on working through my forty days.I kept getting up at three in the morning when it was completely dark outside and taking the train at four a.m. from Thorndale to 95th Street. I had to catch the 5:20 bus, or I would be late and would have to take a re-route. I kept clocking-in. I was the first one there every morning. I usually make the pot of coffee.

I stopped reading *City of God* thirty pages into the book. I kept reading the bus after I closed the book. It was a hardcover. I started the book after I purchased *Richard II* and had to wait a couple of days for the delivery. I had nothing else to read, but had purchased *City of God*. Maybe my mind was on William Shakespeare and I had to look for a placeholder while I laid my hands on it.

The book arrived at home at my mom's. I ran home to my mom to get the book. I opened the package and read the first page and words. I finished the book in a couple of weeks. I was alright and I read a lot. After I finished the play, I read a bunch of secondary and tertiary works. I tried to understand the play differently. I tried to finish what I started. I went back to Doctorow after finishing *Richard II* and read another one-hundred pages. The reading was split.

I tried to finish Doctorow as fast as I could. THe novel takes place in New York City, a place alike and different from Chicago. The book has a slow start, but the pace is brisk towards the middle. I got to the middle part and slowed down a bit. I read in trains and buses waiting to finish the book. I'm still waiting. (I eventually finished it and moved on to the next book. I have a goal, and prayer, to finish 1,000 books in my life. When I start counting, I don't know. I'm not counting. All I know is that I'm reading).

I needed to move fast. Dominican University had already accepted me. I had two more days to move out of my address. This was in the middle of March. I was steadily chomping away at *The City of God* by E.L. Doctorow. I was almost there. Almost done, almost finished with what I had started. I tried fruitfully to finish what I had started.

On the day of my check, as I was approaching the receptionist that worked at Pronto Staffing on the East Side (one of the seventy-seven), I saw a patch on her left eye. Someone must have punched her in the last hour as I was with her an hour before. I walked out to wait for the delivery of the paychecks. She told me to come back since they were not ready yet. I walked to a birrieria on 107th close to Ewing Ave. I ate in peace, a little anxious about my check. I then walked back to the staffing office and picked up my check. There was a second floor in the address building. A second floor that looked like an apartment above the office. Maybe she had gone up there and gotten beat up. But why? And how? What had she asked for and been refused? What sort of help would she ask her? And who would hurt her? Why would then inflict violence against women? Why in the workplace?

The night before, I had taken a stroll in Pilsen. I went to my usual spots. I went to the bar close to Halsted on 18th St. that served wings. I went to eat tacos first at el Coyote, a late night spot open for lunch, I then went to the bar Simone's (with the wings), and then I went to the The Barrel close to the Damen pink line to pick up a beer. (I was praying that the bar Harbee's which had been open for decades would re-open). As always, I was hoping to run into my ex, Gabby. I did not, although I was prudent. Nevertheless, I went to The Barrell and got into a fight, a slight altercation over the South. To be clear, I got into a fight over my home community, South Chicago. South Chicago isone of the 77. One of the 77 neighborhoods that make-up Chicago. It is not the whole South Side. When I say I live in South Chicago, I always get answered with a question.

"What part of South Chicago?"

Believing the neighborhood does not exist, or that South Chicago means the whole South Side, they ask without meaning to cause confusion. It is at these moments that I have to calm my anger, and explain that South Chicago is my neighborhood I grew-up in on the Southeast Side close to the lake, and Indiana.

The girl I was with did not believe in South Chicago maybe 'cause I gave in to my anger and started doubting my own roots. I gave in to the anger I was supposed to feel to look like a fool.

"I'm from South Chicago on the Southeast Side," I said, on the South Side.

"No, you're not," she answered, reacting to my angst and perceived anger. I was three beers in and feeling woozy.

"This is the South Side," she said.

"I mean South Chicago. Chicago is split into 77 neighborhoods and this is one of them. It's on the Southeast Side," I answered.

"This is the South," she responded.

"I think you're confused about where I'm from," I said.

"What would you consider this side?" she asked.

"The West, or Lower West Side," I answered. I realized that both of us were trying to claim our home.

"No, it's not. This is the South," she answered. We were close to Cermak and Damen by the pink.

"I think I would consider the South, South of the City. Anyways, I mean I'm from South Chicago which is close to the border of Indiana on the Southeast Side. Close to 89th and Commercial Avenue.

"No, you're not," she said confidently, shaking her head from side to side.

It was at this moment that I stood my ground, and realized that I had to choose my battles. I knew I had to be smarter and a little wise. I stayed quiet. I looked at her relieved and turned back to the bartender. A few patrons overheard our conversation. I turned back to the right, ordered a Lil Sumpin' and drank slowly. I knew one day, and one day soon, she would drive down Commercial Ave. and not know where she would be at. She would know South Chicago on the Southeast Side without realizing her roots.

A couple of days later, I moved West. I moved to the Lower East Side for the third time. (I had lived in Pilsen two different times in three different buildings or home). I moved to LaVilliata. I knew I was moving back West soon. I moved fast. It was a Monday. I was kicked out of my mom' shoes earlier that day (which meant I was kicked out of South Chicago for the day). When you're not Southeast, you're West. I saved my wages, and gave them up for rent and a deposit. It was a small room in a two-floor house. The attic was furnished as well with a bathroom and renters lived up there. On the first floor lives a family.

I spent a couple of days in hotels. The night before I had walked to a hotel down 87th Street. I had walked all the way past Western, past Kedzie, and California. I walked all the way to Cicero in the middle of the night. I smoked a blunt on the way. I had been refused service and accommodations in another hotel due to my smoking. I told the hotel manager I wanted a smoking room when she asked.

"Smoking, or non-smoking?"

The hotel is on 95th Street a little along the road, but not too far West. She played and toyed with the room keys which she had nicely placed in rows and columns on her desk.

"I'll take a non-smoking," I answered.

"You're not going to be able to get the room," she replied.

"I'll smoke outside," I answered, begging.

"You're going to have to wait twenty-five to thirty minutes,: she replied.

"I won't smoke in there. I'll come outside," I pleaded one last time.

"You're not gonna be able to get it," the slim, balck girl answered me. She expected for me to argue, plead, cause a scene, or just begg until she kicked me out.

"Okay," I said as he looked me square in the eye. I looked down and then away, out at the window. I waited for about fifteen seconds and then walked out. I knew where I had to go. I had to go anywhere, but there.

I moved-in to my Little Village apartment without telling my mom. I moved fast. I packed my bags and moved as fast as I could. I left the North for good. I packed my bags and left in a Lyft. I told the driver I was ready. I forgot my duffel bag packed with my library and book collection. I packed it and then forgot it. I picked it up. I instead went into the kitchen and opened the fridge. I picked up my old wine that was stored in the fridge. I took two swigs, two large chugs. I prayed two times. I then started to take things down. I forgot my paintings/artwork that I had painted and put up. I should have taken them out of place. God let me paint again. I needed to carry *My Antonia* by Willa Cather in my hand. I put it down. I tried to stuff it into one of my bags to no avail. I then put the bags down. I kept on picking things up. I kept on taking things down to the first floor foyer. I waited for the driver to get there. I was counting down the minutes on my phone and the app told me that it would get to my apartment soon. I took three trips up and down. I then grabbed the last things I could, unclipped the front door key from the key ring, and left the keyring with the last of the keys on the kitchen counter. I put the key on the doorknob before slamming it shut. I left it there and walked down. I took the drive. I tried to calm my mind. I took my guitar. I thought it was the most important thing to take. I could not forget it. I made a mental note, a thought springing into my mind every few seconds, for my guitar and its love. My luggage was packed. I needed to move, and I did. I did not regret leaving the North.

I made it past the first day. I made some food. I made it West. I went to *La Chiquita* grocery store. I ate steaks, thinly sliced. I ate them with *El Milagro* tortillas and some sauce my roommate, Gilberto, had. I shared. I smoked. I made it to my mom's in the morning. The Content Test got pushed back until May. I moved around March 15 (2022). I have to make-up with my mom. I have to just chill. I had a lot of coffee that day. I opened up the new canister of *Bustelo*. I have to keep going to her house. My mom. I made my usual offering of fruit and a votive. I ate all the meat I could. Chicken, mostly. I stayed with my mom until my eldest brother M. came in.

I watered the Orchid. It still has not bloomed a second time. It is standing on the kitchen table next to the window. I cut-off the stems at the end following the advice of a planter I met at a downtown plant store inside of a shopping center or mini-mall. (It's the building attached to the red line stop). I bought it months ago in full bloom at Aldi's. I stayed in my new bedroom those few days after visiting my mom. I listened to Warren G., and wrote as much as I could. I did not touch my guitar. It's not alright, I thought. I have to play again. In my memory of my father, I have to play again.

I wrote in my journal:

I'm almost done with *City of God* by E.L. Doctorow. A couple of more pages. I'm thinking of *My Antonia* by Willa Cather next. Or, something else from the Chicago Public Library, "20 books from the past you should read."

I'm afraid I won't have the tools, space, time, or energy to pursue this goal of writing this novel. I don't have a computer. A laptop. I can't log on to the CPS computer from ChiArts I kept. God bless us. I hope I finish and publish. I hope to be done with the novel in the Fall by October.

I need to type it all. I hope to self-publish on Amazon and maybe make a lot of money twenty years from now. If Jeff Bezos is charitable.

I have to write fast. I have to think fast. I have to bless my writing. I have to write under the power of me. I have to write fast. My Grandma died for our sins. God rest her soul.

I kept on practicing what I needed to practice. I kept writing. I kept drinking coffee. I kept praying. I kept praying to the patron saint of publishers, St. Francis de Sales.

St. Francis de Sales bless our writing. Amen.

On the third day of living in the address, I kept on reading. I started *Recitatif* by Toni Morrison. I was reading the intro by the third day. I borrowed the book from the South Chicago branch of the Chicago Public Library. I also checked out the Willaim Shakespeare collection at the library at the time I got the book. I thought at the moment that *Pericles* and *Romeo and Juliet* would be great reads.

I had a feeling that I needed to buy Tp, toilet paper. I felt guilty of spending all the Tp in the apartment and not buying a replacement. I have to be good, I thought. I also had to put on my contacts. That was a recurring thought, putting my contacts on my eyes. Maybe I felt my eyes will be damaged by contacts. I had a strange thought that I had to buy a new pair of glasses. I made a prayer to St. Lucia, the patron saint of people with blindness. St. Lucia let me buy a new pair of glasses. Amen.

It was 1:30am and I was chugging down a cup of coffee. I had to finish it soon, I kept thinking. I had to keep praying and praying. I just have to be me, I thought. A song thought. Write down your thoughts (Mr. Abrams alway said). I had to get my leather jacket back from exchange.

I left it there and we made a trade-off. I had to be careful with money. I had to save and stop spending my savings. I have to be me, and no one else. I had to keep reading. I'm about to get on the road and see the Holy Ghost. (make this epistolary?). I had to buy a small desk and chair for my room. I had to find a way to write. Ihad to find a laptop fast. I had to charge my phone. I kept staring at it as if I did not know what to do. I did everything in my power to be me.

I did not commit to anything other than my education. My God Have Mercy. I see brightness. I see no noise. I hear noise. Amor unconditional, the song says. I was seeing the door in front of me. There was noise upstairs. It probably was Beto (the man who lived upstairs with hsbrothers/roommates). It was over 8pm. I remembered my student Destiny. She's majestic. God bless her.

I was tasting wine on my tongue. A song had ended. I felt a cold breeze through the window. I had opened it a bit as The Bible states. Christ be with us. That's what I pray when I open the window. I heard the neighbors in the backyard.

I smell mostly outside air. I am taking deep breaths. I have to finish the page. I think the world is going on. I think it will continue to run about. I think I have to stay in place. I think I'll be okay. I heard shots outside. I hear police sirens. St. Jude, pray for us. I think I have to keep going. I have to learn to write. I have to buy another pair of shoes. I have to just keep going. I am 34 years old. I am going back to teaching. There's silences. I am going to Dominican University. I am going to start a new Master's of Teaching (MAT) program.

When I was a junior in college I went to The Ohio State University in Columbus. I ran away deep Southeast. I stayed there for a year.

I don't know why I did that. I turned twenty-one there. I should not have gambled.

Presiden Barack Obama was elected while I was there.

The Pond was full. It is a small pond used for celebrations by the student-body. After winning home football games inebriated students jump in in the cold weather. Girls in bikinis jump in, and men in boxers. People get bullied and hazed in the pond as well. During Election night, the municipal police was posted in the pond on horseback. There was no police activity, no violence, just vigilance. There was nothing for the police do to except approve of the activities and monitor for safety. They would laugh along with us, and some of course might have been alumni. I did not jump in, but saw the people that did. People were chanting and throwing themselves absentmindedly. There was celebration and peaceful celebration. I saw kids with "tape shoes," shoes made of clear-packing tape wrapped around the foot more than a couple of times to protect the wearer's feet from cuts.)

There's music. I don't know why, but I think Ihve to keep on writing. I have to write away today. This is all journal writing. I wrote these entries while I was thinking of writing:

I have to breathe. These are page numbers. I'm circling page numbers. This is the fifty-first page on my notebook of three. Fifty-one. I turned back.

(All of this is in first person present because I wrote them as journal entries)

I circled the page number.

I think I have to move my pon. I have to read *Recitatif* by Toni Morrison. Lord have Mercy. I'm not inebriated.

I think there are neighbors downstairs who are curious.

I think I walked through a side block four times. Well, I have to explain this novel.

The Content Test is scheduled, re-scheduled for May. This is march. I have to take it soon. I might have to re-schedule for June. But that is in two months. I'm planning on studying for three weeks.

I have to persevere.

My phone and guitar are on my right. It's a yellow paper.

"Yes, in the past teachers have provided space for me." Solitary space. I think of that image when I think of space. In a full classroom, one can have a silent environment. The last sentence is not accurately written.

I am writing my thoughts. I am thinking of sex.

My mom says forgive. I admire her longevity. I had a girlfriend at Northeastern Illinois University during my first Master's program there. She is from Little village. I am in Little Village now, and saw her before I moved-in. I saw her on the bus stop walking East on Cermak. She's a teacher now at CPS (part-time), and a n adjunct at Malcolm X.

I am holding a teacup on my left hand. I am writing with my right. I am leaving space for breath. I think a female teacher loving a male student is not wrong. I am thinking of a recent case. When asked what she was thinking by a judge, the female teacher answered,

"I thought I was in love."

Who was telling her she was not? She also mentioned that she was thinking as a teenager and as his girlfriend. The first statement seems to legitimize their relationship. But the last two makes the case that she did not know how to be an adult in the relationship.

I think God is real.

The other pink post-it reads, "Yes lots of it." I have to just be chill, and not get bounces around. I need to stay still. I need to pray to St. Jude. I need to breathe. I need to relax. I need to stay strong.

I finished *Recitatif* by Toni Morrison the other day. The two main characters exhibit clues about outer abuse. They both talk about an incident at the shelter, St. Bonaventure. There are two girls. One runs away, and the other stays. They both talk about a gruesome, violent, and harsh incident involving a third girl. The memory of the girl is what brings them together again.

After finishing the book, I checked out and started reading the next day *Richard II* by William Shakespeare.

I have not started reading the play yet. I have opened up the introduction. I have to start it today. My goal is understanding.

The music sounds good. There's noise outside. I hear a truck. I hear the slight skims of traffic. I hear tired going over asphalt. I hear my space heater turning on. I see my space heater in place, small and adequate (I bit my tongue on when I wrote "adequate." I am thinking of my apartment, and the space for the dog and myself. I see my pen. I see a black, broken pen. I see a black pen in a gray outer tube. What do you call the plastic around the pen that you hold? The tube with the ink is called a pen, but the outer casing? The pen's case? I see a black pen with a gray case. I see my towel (white) over two bags (trach, white) of laundry. I see wooden floors, stacks of floor boards. The (coffee with milk or chocolate ice cream- delete or revise9-page 55)

Some areas of the apartment are full of light, others dark, with spots here and there pure black. I see a vertical wall made of brick painted green, lemon-lime green. I see a clock on the wall paused at 11:49 with twenty-two seconds. Is it A.M. or P.M.? It's actually 6:47pm.

I have to listen. I hear a song by Ariel Camacho. Rest in Peace. The song is called *Hablemos*. I hear images of skin, Sacred Heart, and a guitar, a *requinto*, playing.

I have started *Romeo and Juliet* by William Shakespeare. The first act is the best. Romeo seems depressed. He is lamenting, engraving. He might be put to death for loving. Does he love himself? I wish I knew the answers. I must love myself first before anyone else. This thought comes to mind. This axiom does not preclude the effect of tragedy (if tragedy is what we're asking for).

I'll leave it alone. He seems disgruntled, anxious about Juliet who he has professed his love for, yet sad at her loss. There's a mix of excitement,but of loss ws well. There is mystery about his love interest. Mostly, there is tragedy at the betrayal of himself.

Juliet in the play keeps using the word, "hate" to demean herself and others. What does she do to usurp this hate? How does she conquer hate? It is through love.

I like Joyce Carol Oates. I will teach William Shakespeare anyway I can. I have to keep writing. The Content Test is now on May 24th. I am signing up for a CPS internship soon that starts on the 6th of June.

I have a forty of Corona to finish. I am listening to "Red Bone" by Childish Gambino. I have to log-on to the CPS laptop that is no longer active or registered to my name. I have to concentrate on teaching. I have to make the best of my time at Dominican University and graduate.

I have to pass everything. I have to keep writing. I think I am making too much noise,or none at all. I am listening to T.I.I have to think. I have to drink beer. I have to be okay. I have to write more. I almost lost my mom the other day. I ran out the door with my mom in mind. When I got there, I asked, "Why did you not let me see the kids yesterday?"

She had sent me to the left to catch the bus instead of seeing the kids. She was picking them up and I walked to the bus instead of turning right to meet them. I stayed silent while staring at her across the kitchen table. The table was between us. She stayed silent looking down while I waited for an answer.

"You don't have to see them everyday," she answered.

I said, "What does that mean?"

I asked again demeaning myself by making her repeat herself. I wanted to be sure my mom was present and wanted her to do right. I wanted to point out her wrongs. I wanted her to apologize, and tell me that I could visit everyday. She stayed silent.

I looked at the floor while my thoughts wandered 9(and hers as well). I needed to move in grace. il had to pause to recollect myself. I was in anger over our confusion and the lack and use of words. Speech. I looked on while she kept cutting onions. I noticed she was not cutting carefully. I knew her choice of words as well as mine were wrong. I knew I had to visit her everyday, but our words betrayed us. I saw Dr. Duggan one day on the CTA train.

Romeo and Macbeth

I think Romeo is loving dangerously. I think he is submitting to guilt. He is also succumbing to illness. If I was talking to Juliet I would pronounce: You are suppose to elope, not impose your will. (The nurse will tell you you're sick when you're not, and tell you to go home when you're feeling ill).

Is Juliet being abused? William Shakespeare states, "She was weaned" (Act I.3). Does "wean" mean rape? William Shakespeare writes in Act1, Scene 3 "Wilt thou not, Jule?" again and again. The phrase is emphasized and repeated twice.

The oldest book should be read. "So Solomon made all the things that were in the House of God" 2 Chronicles 4 (20).

I have to chug along with the text. I am on Act 1, Scene 4 of *Romeo and Juliet* by William Shakespeare. They are attending the ball, the dance, the shindig to elope with Juliet, and at least ask for her hand from her parents, the Capulets. Capulet has a connotation with St. Valentine. Elopement is the opposite of what the court seems to be planning. Elopement is what might happen later in the play. I think I have to think clearly. I have to fill this page. Rest in Peace, Grandma.

I keep thinking of the 2008 crisis. I keep thinking of our generation, millennials. The Millennials (which I am on the far-end of) were promised the American Dream. We were given this dream by our ancestors in past generations. For Millenials, this dream was taken away, put on pause, and reconverted to something else, something special (a family closeness). We had college degrees, yet no jobs. We all went home with a degree and said "we're here." Only to be kicked out shortly after.

Forty years. That's how many years God gives to wanderers. Those that chose to leave their land under forty will wander for forty years.

We left for college at eighteen,m of course. Those that stayed gained their mothers, or were mothers. Which meant that all kids at eighteen who had left home for college, or run-off, would not see peace in their land. The Bible simply states those that left their land at twenty or under will wander for forty years.

What happens after forty years? God promises you will get your land after forty years of wandering. I can assume the years after wandering will be peaceful. Again, I am assuming at age sixty a wanderer will get his land. What about those that stay in land, and don't leave? They have land.

What if one returns to land before the forty years of wandering? One has to kick someone out of their land to stay. One has to gather a basket of fruit and take it to the place in your land you claim as yours. One also has to take a votive, wrapped in cloth or loins, to their place. After this you will have to pour cement (rocks and grout) on the property, as the Bible states.

It's a strange land (the one you left and want to return tO).

You will have to eat all the meat in your place where you make your offering. You will have to pray in your place for eight days and not come out. After that you can come out.

I have never gotten past the fruit and votive offering. I have never poured the grout recently. Although, I have in the past. I have been giving my mom a bag of fruit and votive for three weeks. I have not stayed in the address to pour the grout, and I have not kicked the people out who I should so I can stay in land. The fruit comes from the local stores on my land, plums, apples, gala, green, yellow) and oranges and mandarins. Apricots as well. The votives are from the local stores as well decorated with religious images, like an image of Our Lady of Gudalupe, or St. Jude with a prayer in the back. Sometimes I get one with a prayer to St. Juan Diego and his likeness in the picture. There's a collection of votives in my mom's address. The votives are lighted in the memory of my niece and who is God and passed away as an infant.

I also lit a votive for my Grandparents who passed away. I placed it in front of a picture of them on the top shelf of my mom's bookcase (filled with photographs not books).

I have to type all of thi. I will read Act 2 of *Romeo and Juliet* by William Shakespeare. I am still just waiting to rise, to pronounce my faith, to look for gold. When I was little my mom used to tell me a story about a dream she had. Her feeling was that the dream was shared with my uncles meaning that they all had the same dream at one point or another.

The dream goes, my mom is back in her hometown, in her pueblo, in her rancho in Jalisco. She is there with my uncles. She is in the main house, a cottage, and by the house is an old tree. It's dark out. It's night. The house, red on the outside, has the indoor lights out. My mom barges through the door. She walks to the big, old, tree slightly to the right of the home. The tree is in front of the house.

She digs with images of gold on her mind. She digs with her hands under the tree. She keeps digging with her face possessed by an urge to find gold. When she gets to the bottom she stops. She gets to a certain point and feels something in her hands. It is shit. My mom used to say you could tell where gold was by the fumes rising from the earth.

Don't ever go to these fumes. My mind makes me think of minerals decomposing underground, metals burning, and creating these fumes.

I saw my dad last when I was eleven. He said good-bye. I stayed in my room. He left. My oldest brother, M., was in the kitchen wondering what my dad was doing at home. He kept pacing to and fro from my bedroom to the kitchen. Envious, panicky, and bewildered.

My dad was waiting to leave. He was waiting to leave because we all thought he would leave. I always thought he would leave. (I never assumed he would stay). I always thought he was my dad because he was. I always respected his music. He was my father who I love.

I respect him. I look up to him. No that

Now. I know that he is with God. His soul is pardoned (I know). He passed on to God. I know he's reaching out to the skies. I know I will be a father one day. My mom treats herself real bad. She also treats, and mistreats my goddaughter. Although, I;ve told her to stop her behavior. She stopped.

Yesterday, M. and her were laughing while my Goddaughter was crying and I was outside. They were both laughing while she and I were crying for her. She is being the best mother she can. I saw God today. I met a girl on the bus. She was wearing all black with blue jeans.

When I was working at Walmart, ten years ago in my twenties, I met a cashier/worker. She was a mom. She is still working, thanks to God. She has a couple of kids. She is hot, sexually attractive. She has a gorgeous, big butt. I always thought I could be with her. She was with me. She is a good co-worker. As I write this, I feel her in traffic driving home to her children.

I always thought I could be with her. She was with me. She was a good co-worker. As I write this, I feel her in traffic driving home to her children. Years later, I saw her again in Hammond, Indiana working at another Wal-Mart as a Manager. She was close to Chicago. I went to the store with my sister, a short drive away from South Chicago.

There's a way to read William Shakespeare. I am in the second act. Romeo and Juliet have decided to get married by the Friar in the play. It seems like a real marriage, a matrimony service by a religious who can perform the act or Sacrament. It seems like an elopement (like it should be). A son and daughter will leave their mom's and dad's home to seek a wife or husband. I think that's the way to do it.

I think your parents will never let you get married unless and until you leave their home. I think you have to be ecstatic to leave home. I have to be ready to leave home and answer God's call to be a husband. I did leave homeplanty of times and came back (a couple of times with girlfriends). Everytime I came back was because I did not keep my girlfriend.

A couple of times they came home to me. I took K. home to mom once. I introduced her to my mom. She carried Ezzy on her lap when she was a baby. She's almost a teenager now. I saw myself with her, and I was with her. She drove away in her car, a Nissan Altima, gray, and I stayed at home.

I wish I would have driven with her to her home. The people on the block, who I guess were in gangs, stopped her car simply because she was black, and furthermore, because she was a woman in an expensive car. They tried to get her out of the car. God bless me.

I saw God tonight. I'm sure I prayed and gave myself life for one more day. I prayed to God today to let me live to the age of 77.

I prayed to God today, like everyday to let me baptize Guillermo Jr. I saw the deacon of my parish, Manny, today at mAss. He was giving the Eucharist. I think I did fine, I think I did good, by going home today. I probably should have stayed longer at my mom's.

Today, March 20, I went home. I also saw the people from my parish. They're all recognized faces. I saw my brother who is a reco. All the people in downtown, where I went after leaving home, are recognized faces. They are familiar because they are from Chicago. We're familiar because we are in Chicago.

I took the number 4 Cottage Grove bus all the way downtown. I then wandered for a bit looking for my friend that I met on the bus. I did not catch her. I went on to the Pink Line train to pray and come back to my apartment. (I was elated). To be honest with myself, I was upset with myself. I was upset and anxious about the girl and sad. I was okay and calm and came back to Little Village to pray. I came back to have a drink. God bless me.

I saw my future outfold before my eyes. I see myself teaching wherever I am living. Teaching on the Southeast Side or West Side. I see myself teaching wherever I am. I have to live where I live. I moved to Little Village to live. My mind is telling me yes, besides all doubts that I will be able to teach on the South Side while living in Little Village. I pray for this to come through. What if I pray for what I want?

Become what you receive. See what you believe.

I pray to God. God let me teach while living in Little Village. Ihave to stay still, I have to stay put. I have to just have faith. Why can't we pray?Why can't we ask for help? God help us. God help the girl downstairs. God help my mom breathe. God gave me this gift. I just have to cherish it.

I went to the labor agency for forty days, got a new apartment, and moved West. I moved to Little Village. I just sayed in the address. I have to live. I have to not die. I have to keep on playing my guitar. I have to just live.

I ended the labor job without announcing I was leaving. I kept walking around the last day, wondering when to leave, and how to leave. I kept on being me. I kept on breathing. I kept on just trying to work. I worked hard like I knew how.

I was always looking to leave. There was a girl who worked at the office. She was in her twenties. She would say hi when I said hi. She was an extravagant girl. She was beautiful. She would say hi when she would walk the floor.

She never really spoke her mind. She just stayed there in space waiting for someone to talk to her. She would let me drink water. I would drink water from the water tank. I would drink three cups then turn and speak to her.

I spoke to her when she got up. I went up to say hi. She would be at my left when i walked-in. I would sip and turn right and say hi. I then would ask about her day. She would always answer affirmatively. She always looked abused. She looked as if she did not want to talk. I always suspected that she was being abused in the factory and at home.

It seemed she would go up to the bathroom and come back abused. Her thoughts, I would hear. She would dissociate. She would not pray, not think, she would walk. I'm sure she would get raped. She would go back to her abuser. She would not get up from her chair. I would mutter "hi" after getting water from the water fountain and walk away. I felt comfort and so did she once I saluted her.

Chapter 32: The Factory

I would rip open one-or-two ton bags of sugar with my blade everyday. I would drive the forklift. I would stand on top of boiling water, sweating, taking off clothes wondering when the next bag would come. I would stand-on the top of the Willis Tower, as I called it, on top of the huge water tanks with scalding water slowly filling while we dumped sugar. We would climb the towers through a ladder that was not hard to climb.

The labor was physical. Sometimes, we had to use a sledgehammer to break apart the sugar. I kept whatever I could to just work. I would see the girl going to and from at times. She would seclude herself in her office. I would open the first gate, garage door to access the compactor. I would throw out the garbage and stare out at the office through the windows. I would at times say hi. I would turn towards the office (away from the field) and walk away. (the field being the main warehouse floor which I would ignore).

I saw her a couple of times. Eventually, I learned her name, Augustana. She was gorgeous. She is gorgeous. I went to work everyday to see her face. Her body is gorgeous. I saw her walk slowly up and down the stairs and hallways. She was always very quiet. She was always moving her booty slowly. I talked to her one day in the back office. She was getting ready to get to Oaklawn. I said goodbye and she got in her car. I later got lost in Oaklawn on 95th Street. I took the bus back there in the morning, later in the morning, around eleven.

I had stayed at a motel the night before. Smoking a blunt on the way, I made it to the motel at one in the morning. I took two buses to get to the motel. I walked out of the first motel after being refused service. She asked whether I wanted a smoking or non-smoking room. I said smoking. She said wait about twenty-five minutes. I said, I'll take a non-smoking.

You can't smoke in there, she said. I'll smoke outside, I responded. I can't give you the room, shesaid. I walked away after staring out and taking a pause.

I then took the bus back East a bit. I walked to 87th. I kept praying. I took another 87th bus going West (turning around) and hit 87th and Cicero. I walked to 91st and Cicero to the Miami Inn. I called my sister the next day (before walking out). I was in the hotel bathroom. (I believe I can grow old on the Southeast Side).

I then walked to a Goodwill store. I bought a pair of beige pants. The Goodwill store was close to home. It was in Evergreen Park. I then took the 95th St. bus going East to Commercial. I went back to South Chicago, one of the seventy-seven neighborhoods in the City of Chicago. I went back home and asked my mom where she was, why hasn't she answered the phone?

"I was at Walgreens with your brother?" she said.

I thought about the day. I needed to stay South. I needed to stay at least South of downtown, South of Harrison on the red Line.

I went home and got kicked out.

Chapter 33: The Factory (part II)

I quit the day I knew I was going to teach. I quit because I could. I quit to (keep) teaching. I quit to fill out this page. I quit to know I could quit and live. I quit because I knew I had to quit in order to pray. Addicted to sugar, I left the factory knowing I would try to live.

I left the girl. I left because she was taking care of herself. She was going through pain like myself. She kept on looking for stability, but most often found something else. She found milk. She told me one day she was going to have cereal for lunch one day.

Milk in order not to teach. The Bible states that we will drink milk like children and not know right from wrong. This will happen when we leave teaching and refuse to be teachers.

I told her, "You always end up looking for more food after cereal."

She kept walking. She just kept looking for someone (most likely her parents) to keep her safe. I kept on looking for her. I kept on trying to say hi. She at times stayed sitting when I would walk into the office. To me that meant she did not want to relate. She made coffee for me once. She got up when she wanted to. She opened up her mind once or twice.

Chapter 34: Tio Daniel

St. Francis de Sales. St. Benito,

As I was riding the Metra, a thought occurred to me: what if I get lost like Tio Daniel? A thought occurred to me as I was riding the Metra. What if I get lost like Tio Daniel? (re-write, re-amplify. revise). I was traveling home to South Chicago, one of the 77 neighborhoods in Chicago on the Southeast Side. I was going to Inferno, the South Side after hanging out in Cielo, what we call downtown, what outsiders and insiders call The Loop. I had gone to church at St. Peter's. Why had Tio Daniel run away? Why had he gotten lost? How had the family lost him?

According to my mom (according to a legend), he was lost crossing the border to the U.S. He had been lost crossing the Rio Grande Valley. He had turned back. He had turned back. Did my family ever cross the Rio Grande? I don't know (I doubt it). People cross over everyday. They are immigrants now trying to cross. Most likely, some will get through. Most likely, they will get caught by authorities, Border Patrol, or what is commonly known as La Migra. Most likely, those that have not crossed before will get caught. Children and women, families from Central America, will probably be housed by our government in group homes, and separated. They will be sent to sponsors. Those from Mexico will get sent back. Most likely, single men will make it across spurred by offers of jobs, housing, and money.

Most likely, they will be threatened with violence. My mom came here to the U.S. in a van. She was in a van with a friend of my Grandmother, another mother. The mother presented the birth certificate of her daughter to the Border Patrol agents. (Birth Certificates like yours and mine do not have pictures). My mom, young at seventeen, pretended to be her daughter and they crossed.

My Tio Daniel is not dead. He did not have a big accident. He just lost contact with his family. He lost contact with my Grandmother, his mother. He lost contact with my Grandfather, his father. He lost contact with his brothers and sister, my Aunts and Uncles. He is lost. My mother, as God is my witness, has three brothers and two sisters. My Grandparents, May They Rest in Peace, have six children. All my aunts and uncles were in the U.S. except Tio Daniel. I have met all of them and grew up with all of them except Tio Daniel.

I prayed for Tio Daniel when I was visiting my Grandmother. I prayed with her for him to come back to us. I prayed that he could visit his mother, my Grandmother, and see my mother, his sister, in South Chicago. I always wondered why there was silence over his absence. I always asked, why? My mother did as well.

My mother kept asking my Grandmother about him. On one occasion, my mother asked outright for a picture of Tio Daniel. There were no pictures. I saw my mom ask for a picture after a visit. I was the only one who visited my Grandmother with my mother. My Grandmother was adamant that the picture did not exist, or that it belonged to her. She must have shown it to my mom. They argued. There was a wooden table in the middle of the kitchen with chairs. They were standing near the entryway to the dining room waiting to leave.

My mom was holding her tongue back. My Grandmother used to hang the picture up on the inside of the cabinet door. A small, long, pantry door. She kept it up there among her seasoning and teas, or taped-up and hung on the inside of the cabinet door. My mom never saw the picture. She kept mentioning it. She kept talking about my Tio Daniel at home. She wanted a picture. She wanted an explanation. She wanted love.

All she received from my Grandmother was refusal to admit the past. All she received were omissions. All she received were _______. I wanted to know why the family chose to dwell in pain. I wanted to know why they chose to just let things be the way they were. I wanted to know (like my mother) why my Grandmother chose not to keep her son. I hope God forgives us all. I always felt like an interrogator when my mom mentioned Tio Daniel. I remember my dad (May He Rest in Peace) dropped-off presents for Christmas one year. He left them on the porch and drove off. He must have made more than one trip up the stairs. He dropped-off at least three bags. My Tio Daniel I never met. Maybe he has a daughter. Maybe he is alive. I remember meeting my dad plenty of times. You only get one dad. I know there is wisdom in fatherhood.

I fell again today. It is March 22, 2022. It means I begged for a woman. I punctured the other side of my ribs. Now the left are hurt, in addition to the right (which were hurt about a month ago). Well now what to do? There is a girl in South Chicago that I've seen every Saturday. I will make her a mother. I need to be close to my mother. In The Bible Adam gives his rib to create a woman. I know what this means. I need a woman by my side to create a man. I ask God to make me a father, and for me to impregnate that girl this year. My Tio Daniel has to be a father by now. He is older than my mom. There are three older brothers and three younger sisters. Tio Daniel is the youngest man (brother). My mom is the youngest woman (sister). My mom (in terms of birth order) came right afterTio Daniel. My Grandparents birthed three men, and then three women. My mom has three boys, and a girl. My aunt has three girls. My other aunt has three girls. My Padrino Jose has three girls and Pepe. My cousin has three girls

(Blanca is her name). My other cousin Mary (from my Padrino) has boys. My sister Chacha has three boys and three girls.

I always had faith and hope that my Tio Daniel would chrome back to the family. I always thought he would make his way to South Chicago like my Padrino Jose. He brought my aunt and cousins to the U.S. while they were young and teens. I remember the small apartment where they lived. The apartment was small, but ambient.

When he came back, I remember he asked about Tio Daniel. His concern for his brother was in the air. He was asking for his presence. My Grandmother, I presumed, waved-off his concern. He's gone, it might have been my Grandmother's thoughts, don't worry about him. But by not worrying and thinking about him, she was making her anger known. Those feelings, those memories, and most of all the loss, and call for him to come back home are real. He is the only one left in Mexico. My mom has her aunts in Colotlan (my great aunts).

My Tio Daniel, if alive, has to be near his hometown in Jalisco. My Tio Daniel might have a child (he has to be older than sixty years old), he might be a grandfather, he might have a wife, and he might want to come back. On the day my Padrio Jose came back, I knew someone was missing.

The fact that my Padrino Jose was here at home meant that there was only one brother (or uncle) to come back home. Where is Tio Daniel? I saw in his eyes Padrino Jose wanted to confront my mom and our family about Tio Daniel. He wanted to contact us. He knew the otus and the light was on him. He wanted to ask.

My Grandfather, was there, in his chair, waiting to speak. He wanted to talk about Tio Daniel. He thought he would resolve everything. My mom visited him a few months later. He talked to my Tio Mercedes and we hung out. They had dinner and talked and talked. What if my Tio Daniel is alive? What if he has a child and lives in a town not far off from where they grew up?

I always pictured him with a daughter, maybe a grand-daughter as well in her twenties. I saw my mom today. I always thought Tio Daniel was living in a small town, a town much like South Chicago. I kept on wondering how her pain created conversation. My mom's pain. She would talk about him dearly. My mom would not talk about him as a kid. She always talked about him and mentioned the accident, the abandonment, and the loss.

Now, I think my Tio Daniel simply chose to not make contact. I think he started his own family. I think he hid and ran from Padrino Jose when he was in Jalisco. I think he just decided to run. He decided he needed his privacy. He did not want to come back. Did he drown or pass away while crossing the border, or did he simply just leave and not come back?

Did he disappear? I'm sure my Grandma told other children something. I'm sure she felt the loss of her child. Could he have gone to her funeral? Strange things happened without talking about the past, and the strange things that occurred in the past out of our control. The past will probably repeat, the saying goes. If you don't learn from the past you'll probably repeat it. Finish what you started.

The strangeness was the silence (immersed forcefully by my Grandmother) penetrated by loudness. The loudness was the will to talk, the need to know, and the right to save. When the silence was broken, the conflict of the past arose, and created a risk that threatened the family.

We could never come to peace with Tio Daniel. My mom especially wanted to understand her pain in order to get through her pain. She wanted family therapy. Most likely she wanted answers. She wanted to know why the family was not using their voice, and making a choice. She wanted to know why there wasn't any action to alleviate the situation.

She wanted to know when he was coming back. I read Lorraine Hansberry and her play "A Raisin in the Sun." It's about family dynamics, the will to survive, and how to get along when the matriarch (Mama) wants to take control (but everyone else is losing control). Walter, the son, and next in line (the eldest) squanders all his money (the family's money) on gambles, and schemes to make more money. He depends on the family to make money, and they throw money at him. After they secure the deposit for their new home, Mama gives the rest of their inheritance ($6500) to Walter to save. But he doesn't save. He buys, or seems to buy liquor, or gives money to his friend Bobo to invest in a liquor store. Mama wants to save the money for their monthly mortgage payments, and put some away from Beatha's school. Her name is beautiful. Her name means pretty. Bonita. The pretty one. Or, again Beneath (a), or Beneath (her).

Beneatha never finds out what her name means, but others go to tell her what it means. As a man much different from her (but who tries to be alike) tries to measure her pain with beauty, tries to measure her beauty, and buy her off through marriage.

Asagai asks her, "Was it your money?" measuring her liver for her deceased father through her money.

She answers, "What?"

He asks again, "Was it your money he gave away?" (Act III, Scene 1, 134)

Beneatha It belonged to all of us

Asagai   But did you earn it? Would you have had it at all if your father had not died?

Beneatha No. (Act III, Scene 1) [8]

Tio Daniel got kicked out of his home only for my Grandma to think he would be back the next day. I guess one day Tio Daniel did not come back and the consequence was losing him. Maybe my Grandmother ran from him.

I think my mom was really close to him. I think my Grandmother most likely separated them to divide and conquer, and that strategy had dire consequences. She probably could not

---

[8] Hanberry, Lorraine. *A Raisin in the Sun.* Vintage, 1994, New York.

unite them through division. The opposite of the intended purpose does not give you the best result.

He never left the address (he just gave into the address). He never left his family, he just kept his family. I never really found out what happened to him. When she was in the hospital the thought came to me to ask my Grandmother about my Tio Daniel. I felt anger and rebuttal in her eyes. She was laying back on her back with her white pillow on her head.

"Your Tio Daniel is Eternal Rest," she seemed to be screaming at me with her eyes.

I never asked. I had the thought of bringing him to the states (for her funeral) now that she was debilitating. I thought these things would come true. I thought he would come to the U.S. with his daughter (if he has one).

My Tio Daniel had to be there by her side, by the side of my Grandmother. God rest her soul. He had to be there by his mother's side. She had to be by her son's side to grant herself eternal peace. I had a vision of him being with his family, and us knowing that he was our Tio Daniel together with his daughter.

I was confident that he was going to be there with us. I was concerned that my Tio Daniel was not going to be there with us. He can come home from Mexico, from Jalisco, I thought as I stared at my Grandma.

Your Uncle is Eternal Rest, she thought without speaking and cocked her head to the left. I sensed her displacement. I sensed that she did not want to deal with these thoughts. The thoughts of him coming back to the U.S. are miraculous.

He sensed that she was passing away. My Tio Daniel soul was alive. I wanted them to have peace. There was a chance he would make it to the U.S. There was a chance my Grandmother had a granddaughter she had not met yet. She was adamant that we stay together how we were together, but I wanted my unity with Tio Daniel.

I wanted and needed to see my Tio Daniel.

Amen. (end of black)

I saw my mom the day of my Grandmother's funeral. I saw the rest of my uncles and aunts. I still had the hope that my Tio Daniel would be there. I saw my Grandmother briefly as I walked the hallway. Her body was laying in rest. I thought about my Grandmother and how I needed to pray with her. Maybe my Tio Daniel crossed once and got caught by La Migra. Maybe once caught he did not turn back and cross again.

He must have gotten scared, lonely, or desperate. Maybe he went back home. Probably, he did not cross twice. He did not make it to the U.S. He is probably alive. He probably is alive with a wife. He probably is alive with a daughter. He probably is alive with a son.

Maybe he was dehydrated. Did he pass out and die on the way to the border (like millions of others). Did he collapse? Did he get left behind? Did the coyotes betray him and leave him behind? He likely did not cross again. He likely has a family. He likely lives in a town close to home. He most likely knows he is my uncle. He probably misses my mom as much as she does him. He probably is a good grandfather.

I had to pray to stay in place. My Tio Daniel was there in spirit. I had to keep praying. I was in the lunch room of the funeral parlor. I stayed there until I felt safe to enter the main room. I saw most of my aunts and uncles. I felt safe in their presence. My Tio Daniel was not there. I went on praying at the funeral. I know he is probably alive and well. I feel him. I sense him. I went on and walked around the funeral parlor looking to get into the main room with my Grandmother and pray with her. I couldn't.

I wish my Tio Daniel was there with me to grieve with me. The bereavement process is hard to go through, but with loved ones it gets easier. Through movement one consoles. Movement is the cure for lamentation.

My Tio Daniel had to know when my Grandmother was passing away. He had to be there at his mother's funeral. I tried to stay calm through all of this. I tried to understand. It seems I have lost many things. I have to know that there is a way to find peace through all of this.

I know my Grandmother has grandchildren she has never met. My Grandmother never met my sister's younger child, my nephew, her great grandchild. She probably has a great grandchild from my Tio Daniel's children as well. All these thoughts are (judgy things) thoughts I should not have. Violence is something I wish we could all let go. My Grandmother is probably in Heaven praying for us.

I saw a resemblance among all of us. I saw that we all looked alike sitting and standing in the lunchroom of the funeral parlor. I saw us resemble a family. I saw that we needed Tio Daniel. What did I want to say about Tio Daniel when I started this story? I wanted to say that my Tio Daniel probably has a family, a daughter, or son, and a wife he loves. He probably has grandchildren. I)probably) have a cousin, or cousin's I have never met.

I wanted to make his presence known. I kept on looking around the parlor trying to find him. I kept on thinking I would be with him. I never saw myself without him. I kept myself in place (while running around to and fro the bathroom) trying to find my space with praise. I kept watching the world go round.

I hope one day I get found and not get lost like Tio Daniel. There was a day when I thought about running like my Tio Daniel. I kept on thinking of myself. I thought of what he might have felt and what he must be feeling now. I think he must feel abandoned. He must have felt confused. He must feel alone.

I think he must have felt abuse. I think he must have felt a flight-or-fight response. Wealth is a ransom for a person's life. But the poor get no threats (Proverbs 11.22.8)Did Tio Daniel have wealth? I am stuck in thought. I went to church today. I made it to South Chicago. I prayed for my Grandmother. I also prayed for my Tio Daniel. I know he hears my prayers. I saw the Deacon who officiated the funeral Mass. I said hi. I said thank you for being there ate the funeral. I tried to sound sincere and apologetic. I had missed the Mass at the funeral home. I had left before he arrived.

He seemed fine. I had seen him tear-eyed earlier before Mass. I later found out during mass that his brother had passed away. He seemed to be lamenting. My Grandmother passed away in January. She was eighty-nine.

"Those who walk upright fear the Lord" (Proverbs 14.2)

My Grandfather who is named Rodrigo Haro (who I am named after) could not walk or stand for most of his adult life. What's in a name? And how will Tio Daniel feel when he meets me? My Grandfather is his father. Will he see my Grandfather in me? How does he feel about my Grandfather?

I am one-hundred pages into *My Antonia* by Willa Cather. THe novel is about her Grandmother.

Proverbs 18.4, "He who finds a wife finds a good thing

And obtains favor from the Lord"

I needed to find someone. I needed to find someone fast. I searched for love. I needed gold, wealth. It is frowned upon in The Bible, but The Lord also grants it to you. Ask for wealth. I think we had to think before speaking. I saw my head swimming in pain. I wrote all night. I wrote a novel called *Content Test*. I typed my manuscript during the day. A novel called *Content Test*. I went back downtown to Harold Washington library. I typed in peace. The library. Books. Writing. Reading. Thinking.

I typed for two hours. The manuscript is in notebooks. I am on the fourth one. This is a composition book. I then went on to St. Peter's Church. It's a brisk walk. I have to breathe

Mostly, I have to walk. I need to order pinatas for the baptism of Guillermo Jr. I have to take a standardized test to become a teacher. A district should have mandatory schooling until age 20. The age when you can stop schooling is 16. We should slowly raise the age to 18, so people can graduate.

Once finished with high school a person has to complete two years in college or university. College and university at the public level should be free. A national, public university (with colleges) should exist. Like the military. The United States University.

These kids can go to college at these universities to fulfill their 20 year requirement. These universities will provide associate degrees and bachelors. If you drop out you will be provided an Associate's. Pensions take care of you as long as you live. I'm getting a borrowed laptop from Dominican University. I need to keep reading. I need to check-out a book from the Dominican library. These are thoughts I need to follow. Mi corazón yo he huido. My God, I think I will write. I have been thinking about sex.

I can make it 'till retirement at age of 65 as a Chicago Public School teacher or college or university professor. That would be 31 years of work, of teaching work, of being a teacher. My birthday of course is in November. 31 years. That is what I need. Maybe, I can split-up my time between being a Chicago Public School teacher, a college professor, and a university professor. I can do ten years at each with an extra year at one of them.

My last name is pronounced in Spanish. That's what I know. My first name might be associated with dogs.

My name was given to me by my mom on the day of my birth. My mom named me after her dad. She wrote down my name on the hospital sheet. My dad jumped in the car when my mom was taking me home from the hospital. My mom always says my dad asked her what she named me when he saw me.

"I named him Rodrigo Haro," she said. My mom keeps telling me he stared at her and asked why. My mom responded to his inquiry," What did you want me to name him, Jesus?"

"Con eso lo calle," she says.

My mom says my dad stayed silent. I don't think my mom understands what that story means when she says it. I don't think she understands the source of pain my father felt. I don't think she knew she was taking his son away from him, and also took all ownership away from him. By stating what she stated my mom did something to all fathers. She took them away from their children. She took away their voice. And I think that is an evil thing. Inhumane.

St. Francis de Sales bless my writing. Amen.

I would have been happy with Jesus. It's the name of my dad. Rest in peace. I would have a different name, but be the same person. Maybe, I would have the same identity. I'm sure I would think of myself differently. I'm the son of my dad, Jesus Perea. Rest in peace. I'm also the grandson of my Grandfather, Rodrigo Haro. I respect them both.

At times I wish I didn't have the burden of being compared with my Grandfather. There is a tragedy I try to understand when I think of my Grandfather. My Grandfather died at 76, and spent most of his adult life in a wheelchair. He raped a woman and was shot in the back.

Why couldn't his life be a comedy? Why a tragedy? I remember visiting him while he layed in bed. My mom was leaning on his chest close to his face. Whatever happened in his life, how he lived, and how he died, I think were all his choices. I'm sure he wanted a different life, but never could reverse time. That leaves me with the Question: But, who am I? Well, I am my name.

Better is open rebuke.

Than hidden love (Proverbs 27.5. 5-6)

Well, when someone is wrong, I do have a responsibility to tell. I think that,

"They said he could have paid my mother money, and not married her" Willa Cather, *My Antonia* (180). What am I reading? I don't think there's anything interesting about *My Antonia* besides the writerly stuff. When Cather writes about who she is reading, she is writing about writing. The writerly Cather brings inspiration. I'm holding down *My Antonia.*

I need to keep writing about Tio Daniel. I wonder if he's writing right now. What seems simple is also frustrating. God bless Joyce Carol Oates. I hope she's writing.

I need more money. I definitely need more. The parents of high school students should have free housing. This is all stuff in my journal. I rode the Pink Line today twice.

I went to St. Peter's. I need to write. I then went to Harold Washington Public Library. I wonder what work Tio Daniel does? A carpenter? I wonder what kind of home he has? I wonder if he struggles with poverty like me?

I have to keep searching for what I am looking for and find it. It's slow writing. My pen clicks , closes and opens. Click up. Click down.

I always thought Tio Danie had a daughter, a grown daughter, college-age. She's probably in college and living with her dad post-grad. She probably went to one of the public Mexican, national or local universities near the metropolitan area by her house.

We can call her Julia.

She's probably driving around her town, or walking in the main plaza looking for snacks or friends to hang out with. She's probably at work. She's probably wearing white, a blouse, and had blond streaks on her hair, like Tia Rosa.

She probably gets along with her dad. She probably lives with him in an apartment in a two-story house (maybe with or without her mom). She is probably an only child, or maybe had brothers or sisters. Maybe she's a mom with babies or toddlers.

Maybe she's single and living with dad on her own. Maybe her mother had her own address. I picture my cousin waiting to work, driving from post to post, and running errands.

I picture her just being an only child living with Tio Daniel. She is probably in her late twenties, or thirties. I picture her mom away. I picture her ready to start a life on her own, ready to raise children (maybe with a small child) and fulfill her promise. I picture her looking for the rest of her family.

Maybe my cousin is closer to her mom's side of the family. Her maternal side is something he rejected. I'm sure I needed to see him come to peace with this. I seem to know where to go. I need to go home.

But how am I going home when I'm trying to conquer my whole world?

I think I'm just looking for a wife. I'm sure by the end of this novel I will find a girlfriend. I'm sure I'll be a father soon. Well let's wait.

I think me writing about the image of Tio Daniel is cathartic.

Gary Moore is cool. The Blues artist. Sounds like Stevie Ray Vaughn. Rest his soul.

I have made a pot of Bustelo. Hopefully, the coffee will wake me up some. Tomorrow, I will donate plasma for about fifty bucks (I have to stop this practice since it affects my physical health).

I have to calm down. I think I'll be able to relax in a minute with my coffee. I just have to slow down. I just have to drink it down.I need some sugar as well, just plain old sugar. Fabiola, Chacha, drinks vanilla creamer which means she drinks coffee. I have to drink a lot. I have to just drink. I have to drink something sweet.

God be with me. I think I'll do fine. I have to learn to cut meat.

I went to a job for one day last week. It was at a restaurant. I went in for training. I had to go back. I had to cut meat. I cut it well. It took me time. I did not go back because the manager was demeaning. I think I applied to St. Peter's, a store called Pete's, as a butcher online. I took the train again. I picked-up some meat at the food pantry at Catholic Charities on LaSalle in downtown. It was close to Chacha's hotel where she works. I found the Felix Hotel right around the corner

Our dad's fake name was Felix which he used to gain jobs since he was considered an "illegal" immigrant by our government. It was the name on his Social Security card he used to work on the steel mills in South Chicago. His name is Jesus Perea. God rest his soul.

I then came back with a bag full of donated meat, chicken breasts, ground beef, and burgers. I heated the meat quickly. I had to finish the novel, *My Antonia* by Willa Cather. I had to eat fast. I had to just be chill.

In *My Antonia,* Willa Cather captures our attention by having the speaker of the novel leave her land, "I joined Cleric in Boston. I was then nineteen."[9] She left her land before being twenty years old.

According to the Holy Bible you cannot leave land under twenty years of age. If you do, you wander for forty years. I always wondered about this. I wonder what will be of South Chicago. South Chicago will still be thriving twenty-six from now when I am sixty.

I left South Chicago for Springfield when I was eighteen. I went back and forth during and after my college years. Mostly, I have lived out of South Chicago. I now live in Little Village. God Bless me. God let me teach. God thank you for life. I have to keep eating.

I keep staring at my phone waiting for answers. I have music to play. "Cold, cold feeling" by Albert Collins (Rest in Peace) is about lamenting. The lyrics "I got a cold, cold feeling"

I'm sure this novel has to be about the (mis)adventures of being a teacher. It also had to be about the Content Test which is in about six weeks 9the fifth one. This novel also has to be about finding my mom . Right now, I have not seen her in over five days.

The Content Test, I have to pass and study for it soon. My test is in May. My semester starts in June. My orientation to the new teacher program at Dominican University is this month in April.

It must be in person, hopefully. Or, maybe it's online. I wrote a weird email today to Dominican.

---

[9] Cather, Willa. *My Antonia.* Viking Penguin. 1994.

I am requesting to borrow a laptop for a month, but I am not registered yet. Hopefully, ti all works out. I have to read, write, and listen. If the test is in six to seven weeks I have to study fast. I have to keep borrowing laptops from the library. I'm hungry. I should not eat after eight. Maybe, I need to stay calm. I have to just relax, read, and write calmly. I have meat. Protein. I got protein today at Catholic Charities on LaSalle. I got to pick three kinds of meat (chicken, beef. And burger) then I was given a bag with a dozen eggs and a half gallon of milk. I threw the half gallon down the grain when I got home. I cooked the meat and stored the rest in the small fridge we have.

The dog that I adopted for a month (sponsored) has heartworm. E has to be on medication for a month. I ate beef tacos. I have to keep my production. I have to keep living. I have to keep watching this show, it's called *Bosch* based on a novel by Micheal Conolly. It's a detective show. I have to study again.

I remember years ago, I stayed in a rooming house on a bunk bed. It was on the South Side. I had a friend there. She was African-American. I never slept with her. She was a student at Northwestern University, but it was clear she had lost motivation. She was mostly in the address and went for a couple of shifts a week at a restaurant. She was poor, but the daily rate to rent a bed (based on the app AirBnB) was expensive. Probably, thirty dollars a day. She and I had no place else to go.

We stayed there until we found someplace else to go. I have to keep writing. It's 9:20 pm. I have to write at nine every night and morning. I need to buy pizzas.

The prostitutes are hidden and never freed.

<u>Tio Daniel part II</u>

I think my Grandmother and Tio Daniel are together. I think they pray for each other. I hear their prayers. They are praying for each other now. Ihave to finish *My Antonia* by Willa Cather soon. On the day of the funeral, I did not mention anything to my mom about Tio Daniel.

I saw her walk-in to the lunchroom where I was hiding with cousins, uncles, and second cousins. She was all black.

"Hi, ma," I said as she got close to me.

I said hi to my sister as well. I said hi to M. as well. My sister was with my kids, and I said hi to my niece and Goddaughter Jazzlyn.

I did not want to see the body. I needed to just see myself feel okay. I ate pizza slices and mini-subs together with a bunch of coffee. I walked back and forth. I walked out once to see if my brother's truck was still on the premises. I ten walked back inside, daid bu to a couple of cousins, and walked out.

****

Break

I am planning on reading William Shakespeare once I finish Willa Cather. I need ten pages. I have ten pages left to read. Right now it's on the left on my desk.

I am thinking of picking-up a new play by him, *Julius Cesar* and *King Lear* come to mind. I have to read one of the major tragedies. I read *Hamlet* and *Macbeth*. I will walk into the Little Village library tomorrow and ask for a laptop

I have to save as much as I can. I have LINk. I have to watch *The Passion of the Christ* by Mel Gibson. I need to watch it now. I have to keep on reading and writing. Something happened to myemail. I got hacked. I'm not getting any incoming messages.

****

Tio Daniel (con't)

My Tio Daniel should be the object of this text. I'm sure I have to chill. I bought hemp the other day. Maybe, I should not drink. I have to slow down. I have to keep going. I have to just cut what I can. I need to buy burger buns tomorrow.

At the end of *My Antonia (1918)* by Willa Cather Mr. Carter kills his wife in cold blood, and quite brutally and violently so that she would not outlive him, and so she would not inherit money, or her descendants. The maternal descendants would not get anything. The matrilineal line would get nothing, and the patrilineal line would get the one-hundred thousand he inherited.

I understood the novel. The novel is about the dangers of not going home. At the end of the novel, Antonia goes home. There is violence in the novel. There is potential for love,but also betrayal. There is a big family, a marriage, and relationships. Girls want to get married to men. Men are looking for girls.

I sense that the novel needed to end.

My Tio Daniel is old, older than my mom. He must be sixty-two to sixty-five. My mom is currently fifty-nine. He is older. He must be wearing a blue, flannel, cowboy, square shirt. He must be wearing blue jeans. He must have an old recognized face like my Grandfather's or my Grandmother's. I recognize their faces in ours.

He must be getting ready for his day. He must be eager to start his day. He must be patient, and dedicated. He seems like my Grandfather's son. He seems like my uncle. Of course, he's a father.

I think he is leading a good life, and living how he should. His daughter must love him entirely. She must be faithful and courageous. She must be a little younger than me, and loyal. What if she has sisters? Older, younger? What if he had nieces and nephews like me?

How old are they? I used to look for answers now I am just asking questions. Why? What is the answer? I am not sure. I have to wonder and pray for my safety, family, and courage to live. I think Tio Daniel will live on in our hearts, minds, and souls.

Hopefully, by writing this Tio Daniel will live. Yesterday, I got an email from my school, Dominican University. I sent a follow-up email confirming my attendance on the 25h for my orientation.

I am excited to be writing. When do I know when the short story Tio Daniel is done? Tio Daniel (short story) is done when I figure out what he means for my life. I think he is just my uncle who I never met, who I am desperate to meet, and who I am interested in getting to know. He is someone dignified, and I need to figure out what he means and how he is part of my identity, consciousness, and family. I have to figure out how and what to write about him, in addition to why. I have to try to stay in this light. I have to stay put. There's a light shining through the window illuminating my page. I have to get through this pain.

When I think of Tio Daniel, I think of him being in the town, wandering, looking for someone, or something else besides what he has. I see him driving his truck, an SUV, black. I see him staring ahead and heading North. I picture him struggling to understand, struggling to get where he needs to go, and struggling to know what he is supposed to be doing.

I see him traveling with his daughter by his side. I picture him traveling with his daughter by his side. I picture him not ignoring life, or his sun. I picture him staying free of trouble. I see my Tio Daniel leaving for work, or knowing that he worked for years and is now care-free and retired. (I got called for a job yesterday at a grocery store. I can work there while my internship starts in June. It is the 10th of April.)

Praise Christ. It's Palm Sunday today.

I'm picturing Tio Daniel going to Church today. I'm sure he went to Church today. I'm sure he went with his family. I thought while walking through this apartment, "I forgot how old he is?"

I keep forgetting time heals all wounds. Now he is old and wise.

"Wisdom bids fear," William Shakespeare, *King Lear*, act II.4.283[10].

---

[10] Shakespeare, William. *King Lear*. Pelican, 2000.

I'm thinking of Tio Daniel going to work. He probably worked odd jobs like myself. He probably has a long-term goal in mind that he fulfilled (career wise). He probably had one job that he worked for and kept for a while.

I am calling for a job (at a grocery store) that was offered to me on Saturday (two days ago). I will probably go to the job for eight weeks until (June 6th) the day the summer semester starts.

I just need rent, phone, and pocket money. I need to finish *King Lear* by William Shakesperare which I borrowed from the Chicago Public Library. I have to finish it soon. It's about a father with three daughters, two of which are married and one that wants to get married. There is infighting between the sisters. The two older sisters don't get along with the younger one and want to derail her marriage. They are treacherous, and are trying to sabotage her future endeavors. Although, the second daughter seems to be on her side when she gangs up on her. They're trying to take her away from her father.

Christ be with you.

"So distribution should end excess" William Shakespeare, *King Lear,* Act IV.1. 69.

King Lear stays with his daughter until death. When she passes away there's nothing else from him to do 9the bickering, the solitude, the fighting is through). He carries her body as a sign that she stayed loyal, faithful, and honored her father until the end. There's nothing else for him to do, but pass away with her. (Does King Lear commit suicide?)

I started a new book, *The Natural* by Bernard Malamud. I will finish the novel. I saw my mom today. I also saw the kids. They are going through a rough patch. I have to stick by their side. God help me live and survive. (April 17, 2022)

The kids are under the custody of my mom. Temporarily, they are living full-time with my mom. I have to stay put. I have to stay by their side while my mom takes care of them. The kids are in her custody fifteen to sixty days until DCFS completes their investigation. I have to stay near. I have to just be clear.

There's no way to end this story. I have to know the end. I know the beginning. I know he is my uncle. I know my mom had a loveable childhood with him. I have to know my part in this story. I have to know where I am. I have to know when I stand.

I have to know what happened to him. There is a way to know. I have to go where I need to go. I have to go to Jalisco. I have to mend my ways. I have to know where I am going. I have to know where I am coming from.

I have to take my mom back to her home state in Mexico. I have to take her back home, and stabilize myself. I have to take her to meet her aunts. (my great aunts). I have to know her hometown. I have to understand what I am getting myself into. I have to be just.

Possibly, getting to my mom's hometown is my rock, the *roca*, I have to push up the mountain. My trip to the past is my rock, my *roca*. The search and quest to find out who I am and who Tio Daniel is the rock I have to push, the *roca* on the road or hill.

My Bible is the New Revised Standard Version. I am in need of The New American Bible which is the Catholic version. When I was at an orientation as a student teacher at The Chicago High School for the Arts a teacher brought a gallon of milk to a meeting. He also bought a box of pastries. I would have bought coffee, maybe a couple of boxes from Dunkin' Donuts.

There are thoughts left unwritten.

My grandmother never asked to see my sister (once she decided she was going). My sister has the most kids in the family, her great-grandchildren did not see her in the hospital. She did not ask for them. She never saw my Goddaughter, Jazzlyn, her great-granddaughter. She could never love herself. I knew she should. Now, my sister had her kids taken away. DCFS gave my mom, their grandmother, custody of them for the duration of 15-60 days while they conducted an investigation. They got taken away from their mother like Chacha got taken away from my mom. To put it rightly, my Grandmother took my mom away from Chacha when they went to Juarez to take a trip.

Christ be with me.

Now, my mom has taken the kids away from my sister. I have been trying to get home.

Part IV: The Break

Chapter 35: The Break

I did not visit my mom for two weeks after moving to Little Village. I moved to Little Village and did not speak to my mom for three weeks until my sister got arrested. I moved-in without telling her where I was moving to. I moved-in and called her two days later telling her I was in a new apartment. I told her I had moved from Roger's Park. I attempted to just explain I was safe. I went home two days later to tell her I was in a new apartment.

"Here are your keys," she said as she threw me my old Roger Park keys at me. She was making a show of it. She was letting me know she was out of control, and by her taking control she was causing (or, trying to cause another cycle of abuse, torture, and pain).

I did not catch (get) the bait. I ignored her (or, at least the act, knowing that it wasn't in grace). I turned to the left and ignored her right away.

I left right away. I moved around the kitchen. I left ignoring her call for ignorance. For the next three weeks, I did not see my mom until she left the house. We should not believe in jealousy. I lived in the room while I tried to communicate with her. I tried to reconcile. I was only in the apartment for a week before my mom cut me off. I kept calling. I kept trying to visit. I stayed on the porch multiple times. I kept trying to write.

After the last time she left me on the porch, I did not go back because she said not to go back. She got desperate, and started pulling herself apart along with everyone else. I did not go home, low and behold, and my mom freaked-out. There was disunity. There was bickering. There was animosity.

My mom arrested my sister (on the third week of me visiting her). I was surprised that she chose to succumb to violence even though she was the victim (and not the perpetrator). My oldest nephew, Dan, chose to not stay with my mom. He is a teenager and told the case worker from DCFS that he wanted to live with his paternal grandmother. The rest of the kids stayed with my mom. She has custody. My sister called me the day after she posted bail.

I went out to find a parish today. I went to Epiphany on 25th St. close to my apartment. I was looking for another parish, but I ended up there. I was looking for another parish close, the one that put together the viacrucis. I went to pray out of a need to fulfill my duty to the Church and attend Mass on Holy Saturday.

After the move, I went back to the address, my home where I grew-up, many times. On two or three occasions, my mom (who with a low-hanging, yet angry heart) told me to get out of the address. I asked her questions about her words, her harsh, rejective words.

I went back once more and the same thing happened. After her conversation when I asked her what she meant she said, "You don't have to come everyday," and she stayed silent. I made a decision to not go back for a bit. I kept asking her, "What do you mean by that?"

I did not go back the day after she said, "You don't have to come everyday." I stayed at home for three weeks accrodign to her (what felt like two weeks to me). I stayed home in my new apartment. I even got a dog. I sponsored a dog who needed a temporary home (to alleviate his symptoms). He had injured his tail, and been diagnosed with a "happy tail." He had a cone over his head to protect his tail from his own bites. I kept him for over ten days.

I walked him in my frustrations and anger. I mistreated him when he disobeyed and pulled the leash when I was slightly mad. I would then walk him upstairs looking to stay calm. I stayed in my apartment and wrote my heart out like Joyce Carol Oates instructed. I went to Harold Washington Library (on his birthday) to type. I wrote what I wrote and went to Church.

My intuition told me to write and go South. But I did not go South. I went West. I went back to my apartment, on one particular day that summer, after Church to take care of the dog. I walked the dog and fed him. I loved him as best as I could.

The dog was a blessing. He kept asking for walks. He never lacked energy. I kept walking him. The dog stayed for ten days. He had diarrhea. I stuffed him with food, and tried to make a home for him. I did not call my mom throughout this whole process. The dog kept asking for my mom. I could not get there.

The dog was my companion. I felt alone. It was an animal, but I needed to be with other people with the dog. The dog needed to be with other animals and people with animals. I really needed to be with the girl. She was a hot volunteer with jogging pants on.

How is Joyce Carol Oates a bad writer if you know her name? (How is a carpenter a bad carpenter if you know him as a carpenter?) This is bad writing. This befuddles. I started reading *The Natural* by Bernard Malamud. It is a great novel.

During this break in studying for the Content Test, going to school, and visiting my mom, I took care of the dog knowing I had toreturnhim. God bless me.

There were no visits during this period. I stayed at the apartment. I smoked and smoked. I listened to a cover of a Mexican song by Julian Mercado called "El Tecolote." There was no communication during this period of betrayal, misery, and unnecessary abandonment. I stayed away. I prayed and prayed.

I did not visit during this visit of Lent. I broke my promise. I did not go every day to visit my mom. I missed a day and it got harder and harder to go back to my visiting routine. I just stayed in place. I tried hard not to accost myself, not to accuse myself (nor be a recuse). I tried hard to male and act of contrition, to promise never to sin again (against myself and Our Father). I tried hard to ask for forgiveness from myself and others.

I tried to just understand that what was happening I needed to endure until the skies told me to do otherwise. I stayed unwise, smoking hemp, and walking the dog. There were only gate visits. I breathed and breathed. I went and left. I was left on the porch waiting for the metal door to open.

The gate. I would make it to the gate, a metal-bar door with a glass running down the middle of it, and wired for the door to open. I never saw my goddaughter. I was left in the cold. I turned back and went down the steps (through the metal gate). There were a couple of these visits. I did fly by visits where I stood my ground waiting to go into my home. There was something inhumane about the act (about my mom refusing to let me in).

There was a way for my mom to stay calm, and also a way for her to lose her mind. I really believed she did not know what she was doing, but she kept doing it hoping for these events to lead somewhere. But where? Tragedy or comedy?I believe I told her wrong. I did not know she would reject me. The gate visits were straining and tiring. They were suffocating. I tried hard to get inside to no avail. I knew I had to stay calm and not react. I had to respond. On the last occasion, she berated me for following my heart.

"Why do you come back after three weeks and think everything is better?" she asked.

I stood still. I stood quiet. I put my head down while she talked. I knew I had to stay silent and be wise. I spoke my mind.

"I'm going to be silent and not talk," I thought.

I stood there for three minutes and then went away. I walked to the bust stop on Commercial. I took my regular route along Exchange neither left nor right to be wise. Call wisdom your sister the Bible states.

I went back the next day and she had made-up her mind that everything was out-of-mind. She had constructed this disordered and ununified puzzle of a world that did not need to be connected.

She needed to find the last piece of a puzzle. She needs to let herself breathe. The gate visits stopped. I did ntp visit my mom for weeks. I texted my sister Chacha. I called too. Then on a Monday night she called and I answered.

"I was in County this weekend. Mom put me in jail."

I paused. I was hearing and listening. I heard a lot of back noise.

"Are you alone?" I asked.

"No. I'm at the impound lot. My truck got towed. I parked the truck on the side."

"Okay. Where are the kids?" I automatically asked.

"They're at mom's. DCFS gave her custody for 15-60 day."

I knew this was temporary.

I did not ask anymore questions. She had punched my mom on Friday four days before. My mom called the cops, arrested her, and she spent the weekend in jail and was released Monday morning. During this time (in the time after I moved to Little Village), I did not study for the COntent Test. I did not touch the Content Test book.

I did not study for this standardized test. I did my own individual studies. I became an autodidact like the great Philip K. Dick (RIP).

I studied my books. I read William Shakespeare because I like him. Other books were suggested by others (like the staff at the Chicago Public Library). I read and studied books like Lorraine Hansberry. I read her play, *A Raisin in the Sun*. Others I read by opportunity, like Bernard Malamud. I don't know. I read. I read vastly. I read Professor Li, YiYun Li, and her collection of short stories, *Gold Boy, Emerald Girl*.

Well it's time to pick up the Content Test again. This time consuming, painful, and biting endeavor. I am taking it again in five weeks. I guess I will reopen them. This is the mideel of March. I have to do my time again and study.

I have to move on and wake up. I have to just move on.

<u>The Continuous search for study and stability</u>

I kept looking at the books in my bookbag trying to make them sing. I took them out and put them back inside the bag. I saw them and knew they were two rocks I had to crack open. I put them on top of my desk ready to read. I knew I had to start studying soon. How do I break the rocks apart? And what's in the cracks? Do I carry them on top once they are broken?

Does it mean I will pass the test once I get to the top? Or, will it roll back down like Sisyphus's rock? Can I roll it to the top, conquer myself, and be triumphant? The only thing left to do would be to go back down and climb back up again.

The test will be a test soon. I have to start practicing and taking practice tests to learn the test. The test will be hard, but worthwhile. I am giving myself one week to read and learn part of the test.

Ariel Camacho (rest in Peace) changed my life. The break in studies has to end. I am reading *The Natural* by Bernard Malamud and like it. I am thinking about the Content Test because, and I am thinking about teaching. My novel, this novel, seems to be going in a direction I am not asking. Is this a novel about me being a teacher? Becoming a teacher? Or, living as a teacher? It is a novel about me living. So, let's live. Live to the skies.

I never tire of praying for my mom. Of seeing her, and of telling her I am okay. She seems to be of sound mind. I kept thinking, "I have to go tomorrow," but I never did. I thought, "I have to play my guitar," and I did. I had to take control. I had to learn to drive. God bless me.

Chapter 36: Tai

My adventure with Tai, the dog I fostered from PAWS, a no kill shelter, went according to plan. Except, I returned him after two weeks. I walked the dog three, four times a day, sometimes more. I gave him all the food I could (except the last day when I returned him in the morning. I didn't feed him right that day. I did not give him a can of wet food, but only dry food and his medicine for heartworm. I even bought him a bag of kibble dry food at Walgreens. The rest of the food was free from the shelter. I walked him and the neighbors noticed me with the dog. I got him more toys from the shelter.

I took him to an alley one day after Walgreens and threw the chew toy. I let him play catch. I let him lose for the first time and he ran for the toy. It was shaped like a bone. It was his favorite chew toy. He ran back and forth for the chew toy and brought it back a couple of times. I smoked hemp while he played.

I brought him back home. I played with him at home too while I cooked. I kept him out of the yard since his neighbors had their own pets. I took care of him as best as I could.

I had read something by Joyce Carol Oates one day while sitting in my room. It was an introduction to *Jane Eyre* by Charlotte Bronte. It is fine.

 St. Francis de Sales bless my writing. Amen.

It's fine. I have not read it before. Maybe, it's been assigned.

This is an actual [art of the Content Test practice book:

"Which of the following would be a good title for the passages?"

    a. An overview of Vocational Counseling

    b. Why Students Need Vocational Counseling

    c. The Duties of the Vocational Counselor[11]

In Jane Eyre by Charlotte Bronte writes, "Nothing, indeed," thought I, as I struggled to repress a sob and hastily willed someters, the impotent evidences of my anguish." (Check

---

[11] White Book, 44.

quote). I have not read Charlotte Bronte before. I have not finished Bernard Malamude. I have to read one thing at a time.

I read Joyce Carol Oates as a young writer. I read her when I was nineteen, or twenty. She was/is the writer I go to in libraries like Lil Simpin in bars. The Content Test I have to pass. Charlotte Bronte I will read.

I put down Thomas Wolfe. I have *Look Homeward, Angel* priced at $1.95. I have to finish both. I have to read actively. There are people around me, real people making noise knowing that other homes are here. I think there are people who never get out of an address because of real physical, mental, psycholigical, and sexual abuse and it gets scary. I think growing old should be admired.

The dog

I searched for a dog from PAWS once I knew I wanted to adopt. I searched for a couple of dogs online on my phone. I found one I liked. His name was Woof. I planned to adopt him soon. I had a talk about adoption with my roommates. I sat on the couch in the living room drinking and speaking.

"I've been thinking about adopting a pet," I said in Spanish. "What do you think?'

"Ahh, I think it's okay," one of the roommates said after a slight silence.

I asked the other roommate. He said fine, shaking his head without using his voice. I picked Woof and emailed the adoption center. They emailed the next day.

"Woof is not available for adoption. But there is another dog available. His name is Tai."

I emailed back. "Sure, I'll adopt Tai. I can pick him up today at 3 pm."

"Sure see you then," a girl named Mattie e-mailed back.

"I went the next day to pick-up Tai. I stood in front of the desk and waited for instructions. Mattie gave me a black folder filled with literature on adoption. There were handouts on training, feeding, and above all medication monitoring. I read through some of it.

"Have you taken a look at the literature," Mattie asked. She was a scrumptious, white girl wearing all balck. She had blonde hair.

I waited a bit, and then I saw Tai. He was on a leash, wearing a cone over his head, and seemed to be cheery. I took him home after they handed me a bag of food and toys. I grabbed the leash and walked him home. He did not know where he was going. He seemed to not know he could go through the doors. He paused and then I said, "Coe on, tai," and we bolted through the doors.

I walked him home with his cone. He looked around the neighborhood. He was excited to go home. I walked him up the stairs and immediately he seemed to ask to go back to the shelter. His eyes told me she was sad. Two weeks later, I returned the dog to PAWS. I gave back the leash. I gave back the food and his medicine.

I did not know what I was doing. The last dogs were violent. I would pull and pull his chain, yank it, so he could calm down. I respected Tai, and he was strong. I did not know how to calm him. I saw him fight to stay in his room. I couldn't keep him still while he climbed on the kitchen table. I could not stay with him without controlling his behavior. I respected Tai and he was strong by my side. I did not know what to do to calm him.

I saw him fight to stay in his room. I could not keep him while he would climb on the kitchen table. He would growl. He would get angry. He could get aggressive. He would want to walk.

Every worker must join a union.

The same day I returned to him, I saw a Viacrucis on 26th Street. I met a girl. God knows she's safe. I met her in the parking lot. We kept talking. I fe;t high. High on life. I followed the Viacrucis to the Park next to the jail. They put the festivities together. They crucified three guys on a hill. I seemed eager to find the girl. I kept going back down the hill to use the portable bathrooms. I never saw her.

Selah means "play on".

The Land said bear arms. They make you put your arms in the air. God help me write. God bless phone and rent.

My mom has the whole day for the kids.

Chapter 37: Easter

I bought candy for my niece at Walgreens one afternoon. It was the day, Saturday, before Easter and I planned to take them home to Jazzlyn (who was staying at my mom's under custody of her care). I bought them at Walgreens along with a bottle of wine. I planned on taking them to her after church the next day. It was a bag of assortments, M & m's, milky ways, and musketeers. I also bought some peeps. I left him in the bag for church.

The next day I went to church. I went to Immaculate Conception. I walked all the way to my church in South chicago. The mass was lively. I carried the bag towards the bus stop. I missed my niece, my Goddaughter, dearly in addition to my sister. I walked around Commercial Ave. looking for a way to get home. I could not get up the stairs.

I walked to McDonald's praying to God to let me see my mom (in addition to Jazzlyn). I eventually made it on a bus after spending some time at Walgreens. I went to two stores. I went to a grocery store called 1st Choice and bought a packaged cold sandwich. I also bought some packaged prepared mangoes. I also bought a cup of orange juice which was extra sweet.

I waited for the bus which was taking too long. I stood around the store waiting to act, waiting to decide whether I should see my mom or not. I went to Walgrens to make an appearance thinking maybe I would build up the courage to go home. I was two blocks away.

I brought three chocolate eggs. I then procrastinated on paying, and did not walk-up to the register. The security guard checkers-up on me a couple of times. I eventually talked to the pretty cashier and checked out.

Walked to the bus stop and took the 95th bus going West on 92nd and Commercial, Imade it to the Red Line. I gained no entry to my mom's house that day. I studied for the Content Test. The next day on a Sunday, I visited my mom. Iknecked in her door the next day after church. I attended Mass at St. Francis Assisi church on the UIC campus. I then medemy way to tmy mo's. I lied all along Roosevelt Ave. until I made it to the Red Line. I knocked on the door and she handed me a credit card I had ordered. I then kept going to the Red Line. I struggled to get back to Little Village. I felt I did not see Jazzlyn for the 10th day in a row. My Brother M. thinks he's me (he thinks he baptized her). I did not see my baby nephew who I am baptizing soon.

I need to study for the Content Test soon, again. I have to just keep studying for it and gogn home. I have to keep going and I am. Tomorrow, I am going to attend my Dominican University Orientation. I will log on from my old university, Northeastern Illinois University.

I have to keep scheduling my practice exams and study for the Content Test. I have to also schedule my visits. I have to pass it soon. I have a month to pass it and conquer it. I have to conquer it a piece at a time. I have to study and open the book.

I have to keep on trudging along. I have to pass it, and keep on visiting my mom. I have to know my Content. I have to know how to stay with my mom. And why? The Content Test will be conquered one day through praise.

St. Francis de Sales bless my writing. Amen.

I have to hide and study and write. I have almost completed *The Natural* by Bernard Malamud. It's about baseball, a girl, accidents, life, fatherhood, and the will to survive. There's a girl named Memo (why she has a male nickname, I don't know. Maybe her name connotes a message. Did you get the memo? Her name is a shortened version, a nickname of the Spanish name Guillermo. But she's a girl. There's also an Isis. There is a guy, main character named Roy, who I admire and look up to.

I gave in to the COntent Test and studied it again. I completed the novel by Bernard Malamud, *The Natural.* It ends tragically, but he lives. I enjoyed the end. I mean he lives, but breathes. The Content Test is scheduled soon. I will be ready, prepared, and enthused. It's a requirement to teach and I hope to pass it fast.

It's the same material. I have studied it before. I have two books although I could have three. I have to acquire the practice test online provided by the ILSC company which is run by the state.

I got into the new orientation at Dominican University. I found out that the English Language Arts placement for our internships will be at St. Patrick High School on the Northwest Side. I look forward to working with them. I have to save money for a suit, and get ready for the semester. I also have to apply for a job soon and turn in my shot record.

I have to finish typing the short story about Tio Daniel. I applied and accepted a job today at a staffing company. The staffing company placed me at a meat processing plant. It's a pork factory. I accepted the position right away(after being offered a job at my old processing plant packing chicken). I'll start tomorrow.

I was nervous. I was nervous about everything. I knew I needed my boots. I knew I had done good work before. I knew I was going to show up. I knew I was going to go to Orientation. I knew when I had to go to work. I knew I had to pray. I knew I had to go home and then work.

The job was going to start soon. I knew I had to pray to St. Josaphat. I knew the job was going to be hard. I knew the job was here. I never thought I would see the day when I would write. There's a rule about writing. Write like a character not a writer. I have to write like a protagonist. I have to write like a speaker. I think I have to write like a protagonist.

I published when I first entered graduate school. About ten years before being admitted to Dominican University, I wrote my first story for a journal, *SEEDS.* I published again a few years later. All the stories are part of *Gangero,* my long-running novel (in series), I published a bit at a time.

I published for my mom. I published "Report Card" my first story, then "Tom and Jerry and Pancakes" which I took home. I also published "Springfield" about my college years. The journal staff had a ceremony fro "report Card" that I attended. I earned a certificate for publishing, a prize that was not available to everyone else. I also saw my William Shakespeare professor at the reading. He had a story published in the magazine. I took the magazine home. It was a long way home from Northeastern Illinois University. I took a late-night bus and trekked all the way home, South.

All the pieces I wrote and published I took home to my mother. Some I published later.

I published "Tom and Jerryand Pancakes" for my mother. I published it multiple times. The final version I edited for my English Education class. I revised the whole book, the whole novel. "Tom and Jerry and Pancakes" is part of the novel and I wrote it three times.

I presented my short story to the class. I read it out loud. The book, the published journal in book form arrived at my doorstep a couple of weeks later. I sent the digital copies to my brother and sister. I also showed the hard copy to my mom, and dedicated the story to her.

I published "Springfield" a couple of years later when I was at the end of my teaching degree experience. "Springfield" was published in a book-form journal as well, *SEEDS*. I showed it to my family. I also forwarded the digital copy to my sister for her birthday. I sent it to her. The hard copy I showed my mom.

I also showed my mom the books I published on Amazon. The first collection of short stories, I dedicated to my niece Penelope Giselle Vitela who passed away as an infant. Eternal Rest. I showed my mom that collection and my first novel *Gangero* as well.

I went home with these publications. I wrote a chapter called "Content Test" which I turned into a short story. I shortened and revised this story. Some of my stories had been published in *SEEDS* by the literary journal of Northeastern Illinois.

"Content Test" was a new short story. I submitted it for publication for the Spring Issue. I heard back from an assistant editor with a commented copy of the story. I sent them back the copy with my changes in a Google Doc.

I wrote a message, "I appreciate all the work."

I never heard back from them. They published the journal without me. I had submitted, and they had accepted and published three other short stories in the journal. They published it without telling me they were refusing the story. They left me in confusion. They never responded, but rather reacted. I don't know what their thoughts were or are. I don't know their aims, or how the situation unfolded. All I know is that I have to respond by writing. And writing well.

Write well. Write your thoughts.

I thought about publishing elsewhere. I have to choose another journal. The journal is run by Yiyun Li. I have to read. It seems a viable place to publish. I will have to publish next year which is the next submission cycle. Or, I could publish as soon as possible to another journal taking submissions. I have to find a journal soon. I have to find a journal that is caring. I journal where I can submit, grow, and emerge as a writer. I have to find another journal. Dominican University has to have a journal. I have to check out the English Department. I have to keep looking for somewhere to be. St. Xavier might have one, or UIC. But the odds are I will be published at Dominican soon.

I think writing a reliable narrator, or writing like a reliable narrator, is hard. Maybe a n unreliable narrator with a tone that questions instead of answers would make a better narrator. I am writing. I was thinking, "I will write soon." There is something agonizing about Northeastern.

I have to write a novel on the university. Maybe, this is that novel. Have I written about Malcolm X College and my time there? I don't think I have written a whole piece. I have to write a good novel about Kalpesh. Perfect Art. Art is a friend from college I met in Springfield. He used to drive a box-shaped car. Maybe about Akram and the other Indian neighbor. Maybe, I have to write a novel about the frat, abit Alex, Brandon, Patty, and Courtney. St. Francis de Sales bless my writing. Amen.

Maybe, I have to write about Adriana Benitez, Daisy, Gabby, but above all I have to I have to write about that girl. She was a hot one, friend of Glady's, who aspired to be part of the co-ed fraternity, but was pushed back by its animosity, it's backlashing and backstabbing, it's gossip, and by too much talk. She needed to be loved. She had a gorgeous body. I missed La Chiquita.

I miss and remember another girl that was always on the Huskie bus going to class. I remember her. The other girl that hung out around the frat only wanted to hang out. I remember Gabby gave me a cake for my birthday.

I have to pass the Content Test. I have to find a way back to the frat. Maybe, I'll just say hey. I slept over Alex's home once in Melrose Park. I remember we smoked a bunch of hemp.

I have to learn to get along with the world. Is this a novel, or a journal entry? I think I can rite poetry like Joyce Carol Oates.

I love

The dove

Inside

I should write a one act play as well. I can write a play like Lorrained Hansberry. The world has to perform the work of Joyce Carol Oates and read the major works of this American writer.

I have to write and write in Spanish.

I have to write. Maybe, I can write in Spanish. I have to publish "Tio Daniel" (short story) in a journal. Maybe, the journal in Dominican University will publish me. I have to remember Ana from Apsi. I went to Illinois State University. I remember I kissed her. I then slept over at an apartment of a friend. The friend was someone I had not met before. Ana texted me in the middle of the night. The girl was noise enough to let me sleep over, and was waiting for sex. She cried. I needed to make love to her while she cried to her parents.

I looked at the text from Ana.

"Are you alright?"

"Yes," I responded.

She called and I told her I was safe. There was a Latina and balck girl in the apartment. They were roommates. There was a laptop on the living room table.

"Don't use that laptop on the table. It's my roommate's," she said as I laid ont he couch.

I remember the girl. I made out with one of the girls. She was another girl not related to the girls at Illinois State University. They came to Deklab, wherel went to school and had an apartment, for a party. They were from another university, Lewis University. They came to our private, unofficial farta house. THe house was coed like our fraternity, I also remember Liela. She;s sexy. I checked her out a couple of years later. She's a mom now.

St. Francis de Sales bless my writing. Amen.

I have to come to peace with APsi. I joined the co-ed fraternity my first year, my first semester at NIU (Northern Illinois University). I eventually graduated from NIU. I even found a girlfriend in the frat. I enjoyed my time.

I went high to their recruitment meeting, and did not find my place. I did not know where I was. I had soaked weed that was highl;y potent. I met people. I remember a beautiful girl with blonde streaks who toal me where I belonged. She asked me, "Are you okay?" and grabbed me by the arsm.

She told me to stay in the group. I did not understand what was happening, but I knew I was there. I was talking and surviving.

I eventually went through the whole recruitment process and joined as a full time member. I did not get much sleep. My grades suffered because of time management, and events through the frat.

I joined the Fall who I met in the frat. They are my brothers and sisters in the fraternity. I did not see them much after graduation. I tried to hold on. I rejoiced and rejoined looking for safety, and friendship. I kept praying. I went to the Newman Center in Dekalb, the small church from the Diocese of Rockford on campus. I went to Mass almost every Sunday.

I met one of the girls in the church that hung around us. I had a job in the computer lab looking after students and the lab. I refilled paper in the printer and shut down and opened the lab.

I'm listening to Lil' Peep (Eternal Rest). I think he was a great artist. Today, March 29, 2022i is the date of my niece who passed away at eight months.

<u>Tio Daniel</u>

I have to take my mom to her land. It has to be this summer. I have to offer the trip. I will baptize my nephew soon. I will be a father soon. I will have to breathe soon. I will be a husband soon. I will be a teacher soon. I will be a homeowner soon. I will find Gabby Anaya soon. No one knows what is going on.

I will have a car sson. No one knows what is going on. I have to think of my Tio Daniel. I think my novel will go in the direction I take it. Am I going to be a teacher? A deep thinker? Or, a speaker? Am I going to keep smoking weed? There needs to be more characters. Clarissa, that's the name of the daughter of the protagonist in my short story "South Automotive."

I have to construct what I want to construct. I have to stop smoking hemp. I have to be clear. I have to be powerful. I have to do everything in my power to just breathe. I have to just write, and write, and write. I have to know where I am. I have to just go out there and be me. I have something to do. I have t things to do. I have to study for the Content. Test. I have to just breathe and type. I have to focus, and focus one me. I have to keep teaching and writing.

<u>Tio Daniel (new section, page 153)</u>

I'm sure Tio Daniel walked around his town looking for girls. I'm sure he looked for one woman. I'm sure I do the same at times. (I have to go where I need to go). I'm thinking of his wife, and the life he led. I'm thinking of his wife, and the life he led. I'm thinking of his Church. I'm thinking of the word "lost." That's what my mom always said.

"Perdio," she used to day. She used the word.

"Mi mama dice que se perdió," my mom would say, or a different version of the sentence, to put the meaning across that he is lost.

Showers. I need showers.

Well, this is the construction of my idea (s), vision, or image of my Tio Daniel. They might not be true. They might be my ideas of his life. The idea of him being alive is a possibility. He might not be dead. His daughter. I hear his daughter. I think of St. John Paul II a lot. The truth might not be thri truth. The truth of my Tio Daniel is a buried secret. The truth might be divisible. I hear my thoughts, They are screaming out. Slow and steady.

I studied all the old study books for the test. They're all outdated. Some of the questions on the test are in study books. I need to go to work soon. I have to take care of my eye. These are just my thoughts. I have to take care of my eyesight and get a new pair of contacts, or, eyeglasses. There's another step to passing the Content Test and that's studying. Another is time management, and the last is actually passing.

My life is crazy. Overwhelming, overcoming, over indulgent. I saw a girl today ont he road. She was pretty. She had burgundy hair. I kept walking neither left nor right. Call wisdom your sister. I have to stay calm. It seems there's a way to just breathe. I have to praise. I have to just breathe. I have to just eat. South girls suit me just fine. (A wise man wrote the last sentence). There's a guitar tuner in my left hand. A pen on my right. My sister, I saw the other day. Sh'es pretty cool. I saw my goddaughter too. I'm sure I have to write. I have to breathe. I have to breathe.

I need to be wise. Just run when I want to run. Run. I looked up the proper use of "just."
just adjective \j"est\ 1. Having a basis or conformity to fact or reason. 2. Acting or being in
conformity adverb 1. Exactly, precisely. @. Archaic variant of Joust (2022 Merriam-Webster,
Incorporated. 5/5/2022/ published online). It can also mean righteous according to the same
dictionary. There's a way to Exchange.

Maybe, the Content Test doesn't mean going home to mom. Maybe, it means moving on.
The Lord will look in favor when you find a wife. He will also judge. He will be just.

Exchange is my mom's home. It is where I was raised during my teenagehood. I was
also raised in a small apartment in the four apartment home. People need to write. I'm paying
attention. I'm reading twice. There's no way I can't make it back.

I don't want to have fights. I have to stay calm. I think I have to just breathe. There's no
way I'm going to fail M.A.T. again. I need to just breathe. I need to smoke a cigarette. I need to
just relax. I need to clear out my lungs (thoughts) and breathe deeply. I have to figure out who I
was, and who I am, this king of myself, grateful to be alive. I have to find my friend. My older
coworker. Maybe, she'll be fine. I think everything will be fine. I have to contact her. I have to call
the office number, and hope she answers. I have to ask her out on a date. I have to keep going,
walking, and standing. I have to call the office number and hope she answers. Aloof, this is
chicken scratch. The title of this novel is Content Test. The actual Content Test will be in less
than a month. I have to study material. I need to flip a page.

Philly cheesecakes are one. God let me keep writing. God let me find my guitar. God let
me pick up my check. I need to find that girl. I need to breathe. This Content Test thing is too
much. At first glance, I have to eat more. I have to just breathe more and more. I have to just
breathe.

My mom who I have to find and then run. I might stay unsingle soon. I'm sure it's my
mom I have to find. Or, maybe consummate a relationship, or have a wife the third way (I read
Issac, The Holy Bible.) There's this girl. I call cheekies because she's smiling in the picture.

She's on the cover of ILTS (the book title of a study guide published near Chicago). The complete title of the book is *ILTS Test of Academic Proficiency (400).* She's to the left of me.

First person. The novel has to be in first person. But how do I know what is going on? What will happen tomorrow? This is a journal entry in a novel. My name is Rodrigo Haro. Get up.

"My Grandaddy's a legend," Kendrick Lamar rhymes. A line before she says, "i was born in '87." I was born in 18987 as well. I'm sure my Grandfather is a legend as well if I am named after him. I guess I am the protagonist. Can a portrait be a self-portrait of the artist painting? Can I write a novel about writing a novel?

What does the genre ask me? Look up Dr. Bradley Greenburg. I have to just opus. I have to lose myself on the poage. I have to just breathe. I have to be a father. I have to get Ruby pregnant this year. Damn. I have to stay tune, and put.

Gaining a computer has been an ongoing battle. Keeping equipment has been tough. Saving for a computer has been hard.

I'm reading *The Ox-Bow Incident* by Walter Van Tilburg Clark. I'm reading slow. Croft narrates well up to a point of danger. He writes the "n" word a lot in addition to the word for the opposite of Heaven. It seems contradictory. I have to read closer. (Thomas Wolfe and William Shakespeare are on my drawer and desk. *Look Homeward, Angel* and *The Winter's Tale.* There is an image of the Virgin Mary on the cover of *The Winter's Tale.* I heard of a writer who won the National Book Award, Ibram X. Kendi. His book is *How to be an Antiracist.* I also heard of this other writer who wrote a book *Reading While Blakc* by Esau McCunely. I have to read both. I have to read the National Book Award speech by Ibram X. Kendi. I have to retire at age 65. The summer when I'm 65, I will have to retire. Mexican American Studies, Latino Studies, LAtino and Latin American Studies. I have to write about The Content Test. I'm not numbering pages. I am just reading. I have to stand. *Stamped from the Beginning* is also a book by Ibram X. Kendi that won the National Book Award. I have to get the plot of Walter Van Tilburg Clark (RIP). There is a main character. The narrator, and other characters, there is other plots and actions. There is a trial of bad people. The people are Jimmy, Ma, Gabe, the narrator. The setting is jail, and the train station.

In undergrad, I minored in Latin American dn Matino Studies. I took classes in my studies with a professor from Brazil. Also one from Mexico working on his Ph.D. dissertation. I also took a Latin American Studies class at Springfield. I saw a film about indigenous people. I need to keep writing. I need to keep studying Latin American and Latino history. I have to keep studying. God let there be more food at Chicago Public Schools. God let me relax. Give me the Pow (er). I don't think I give. I don't do you. I don't do you. I have to study hard. I have to stay still. I should have studied more Latino Studies. There's something about Ph.D. I have to go to South Chicago immediately. I have to just stay and breathe. I always admired people with doctorates when I was in school. I always wanted to get one. I enriched myself with self-study. I read everything that I could. I wrote everything that I could.

I tried to get one (a Ph. D). When I was admitted to an M.A. program, I thought about going to my Ph.D. I never did. I am going to get a Ph.D. later. I once told my cousin the plan and she laughed. I have to study English or Literature. Latin American History. I also want to eat. I have to get my degree after teaching.

<u>Reading Journal</u>

I need a plot. Where is this story going? I think I have to have more action, dialogue to move the story along. An outline would be good. I need to do something for myself and the novel. The novel needs another chapter, a final chapter. I might need to keep writing and writing. I need to write for a whole year. One year. I need to breathe and feel alright. I need to listen to Kendrick Lamar.

I have to wake up and be free. I have to jump, and go to Mass. I have no choice. I have to breathe. I have to imagine that everything will be alright, and breathe. I have to control my actions, emotions, and thoughts. I have to say hello and just breathe. I have to know what I am doing, who I am talking to, I have to be safe, and in good health and wellness. I have to know when to stop and when to start working on something else. I have to be me and breathe. I have to stay present and not (un)present.

"I needed time alone with my own thoughts," writes Kanye West in his song. The need for solitude, reflection, and meditation. I think I need that now. The pressure to write is too great. I need the plot of *The Ox-Bow Incident* by Walter Van Tilburg Clark in three sentences. I need to keep reading *The Holy Bible.*

"He is my rock" (sings Psalm 92.16). I have to think of lmy literature. Indeed to get a Ph. D. and in order to do that I need a Master's. The M.A.T. Dominican University provides a way. I have to get studious. I have to just pray. I need to know what to write. There is a way for me to just relax, I have to finish the novel. I have to graduate and get my P.E.L. and E.S.L. at Dominican. I have to be careful. I have to pray. There is no other way for me to stay pure. I have to pray for my family, for Danny, and most of all for Jazzlyn. I have to writer Gangero (II), a novel. Or the third revision. Or, maybe it's best to leave it alone. I can get into the University of Chicago if I try. I can get a Ph.D. I have to know where. I have to get it in English or Education.

I have to get going. I have to finish my wire. I have to relax. I have to talk to every girl that makes eye contact. I have to breathe.

Mom is a voice. I hear her all day. I have to get Gud a swisher. A good one.

I have to get a girl. I have to get a girlfriend. I have to ginish taking care of myself, and part of that is sexual health. I have to have srx with women. I thin part of the novel has to be about my sister and my mom. It has to be about the relationship between them. It has to be about a relationship. I am not part of and am outside of.

This is conflicting. I have to breathe. I have to relax. The last two sentences are meaningful. I guess at success. No wonder, I regress. I hold dear my grand-dear, Eternal rest.

Name one thing you know about Bella. The will to survive is there. St. Joseph, let me be a father.

Part V

Chapter 38: Malcolm X College

I had an interview for Malcolm X a year before I accepted the job. In that first interview, I did not receive the job offer. I got the job a year later. I interviewed with the same coordinator. I spent one successful semester and a year at the college. I tutored and got along well with most of the staff. I met a couple of girls the first semester. I met students who were interested in being with me. The first semester I was lost in my teaching. I tutored what the students wanted me to teach. My first teaching experience (professional) was a success. I met a friend, a girlfriend. Although, the year before, I lived with my mom and the second semester and year I lived with my sister.

Joe-Part 1

I lived in South Chicago at my sister's apartment and at Pilsen the second semester. I met another Latina who tutored with me. She was the only Latina in the Tutoring Center. I met her on the first day. She was someone meaningful. She had luster. She was brilliant. She was to the right of me in the office. I had to just turn and say hi. She was optimistic. She was religious, spiritual. She was an ordained minister at the church in her denomination. She majored in theology as an undergrad.

I also met a professor who tutored in the center, Dr. J. He had the front desk. I always looked around. I saw another tutor right in front of me. I saw another tutor who was married in the corner. I also saw Mrs. F. who was a grandmother and worked as an ESL tutor. There was another wife. She sat right in front of me. She kept telling me to go back to my sister. She told me to visit my mom often. She told me to seek more support. This was my friend, Joeana.

The wife was a writing tutor who had taught before and moved to Michigan with her husband. She always told me to write. She told me to graduate. I was working on my first Master's program. I never finished my first Master's. I was going to go ahead and graduate. 2nd year.

The second year, I felt fine. It was the first year all over again. I worked in a new building that the City of Chicago built. I went to the building with a Counselor Center. I was offered services, but refused to go. I eventually quit. I went to a meeting with the new Coordinator three times. He was relevant to my career there. He was worried and concerned about my behavior (or, lack of behavior) with the rest of the staff. I appreciated my time with J. May God bless her. I consider her a true friend. I had a new office space. I kept teaching even though everyone told me to stop.

She never upset me. I held my phone one night (while texting). I texted back and forth.

The Second Interview

I went back for another interview after I quit. I went back to the same place, teh same people, and the same atmosphere. My Coordinator was missing. She was not there. She must have quit. Someone told me that she went back to finish her degree in education in another state. I never reacted the way they wanted. I never blew up. I never gave in. I just left and then reappeared. I kept on having hope.

The interview went well, but I knew this was just another (mis)adventure. I knew I could get back my job as long as I tried. Life laid in my hands. I tried hard to just keep working, and to work everyday. I went in for the interview and felt at peace. I never got my job back. Due to lack of communication, I could never relay that I needed my job. I could have blamed others, but I knew everything laid in my hands. I had an interview with another coworker who had a promotion. She was the new coordinator. She had a successful interview with me, but didn't hire me.

I got a new job after being admitted to Dominican University. I got my first two checks on a Friday. They were long overdue.

I believe in God and I believe. I have to pray for my faithful departed souls of my niece, Grandparents, and my little cousin (Eternal Rest Grant Unto Them and Let the Perpetual Light Shine Upon Them). I think I have to pray for every one of them. I think I have to pray for my well-being, and the well-being of those around me.

I think I have to be fair. I have started a reading journal to understand and interpret what I read. The plot of *The Ox-Bow Incident* by Walter Van Tilburg Clark (Eternal Rest) is finalizing. There is atrial at the end. I need to understand the end. I need to know what is going on. I need to move on to William Shakespeare and *A Winter's Tale*. I have to know my texts. I have to just focus. I have to breathe. May God bless me, forgive me, hear my thoughts and prayers, and always watch over me. Amen.

I went back for another interview a year after I quit. I went back to the same place, the same people, and the same atmosphere. My coordinator was missing. She was not there. She must have quit. Someone told me that she went back to finish her degree in education in another state. I never reacted the way they wanted. I never blew up. I never gave in. I just left and then reappeared. I kept on having hope.

The interview went well, but I knew this was just another (mis)adventure. I knew I could get back my job as long as I tried. The future lay in my hands. I tried hard to just keep going to work everyday. I went in for the interview and felt at peace. I never got my job back. Due to a lack of communication, I could never relay that I needed my job. I could blame others, but I knew everything laid in my hands. I had an interview with another coworker who had gotten promoted. She was the new coordinator. She had a successful interview with me, but didn't hire me.

I got a new job that day after being admitted to Dominican University.

The last comes first. At times. Sometimes.

The fist comes last.

I hear shots. I am puzzled. It seems gangs are shooting. I think hitting a full home run is possible, it's a possibility. It's one of many outcomes. Hit. Out. Flyout. Home Run seems far and distant. God let that guy stop shooting.

I think it's possible. I won't get hurt in Little Village. I think it will take a lot for gangs to give up their land. Where do you work? Is the most common question. Well, I'm going to (achieve), attain, and acquire my Educator License with Stipulations (ELS) on August 1st- the birthday of my faithfully departed Grandmother. I have to write, and be calm. I have to just try to be still. I had to take a shower.

I'm not sure what getting my teacher license on my Grandmother's birthday means. Maybe, ti emans I will get my license to teach and pray for my Grandmother. I will have to teach a provisional license for two years. So, I will be teaching on a educator license with stipulations for two years. I need to think of things to improve on. Some areas are hard, others are not.

I left my friend and kept seeing her around the neighborhood. I moved into an apartment on Blue Island and 23rd. I kept going up and down. I went to work and back. I never talked to the neighbors. They were still. I just heard their voices. I heard their voices. I never talked. My landlord was Christian.

Joe

I saw Joe again on the Cermak bus. She was heading to the Red Line, or maybe somewhere else. She got out of the bus fast. What is this writing about? My time at Malcolm X College tutoring and teaching? Or, is it about Joe (my friend) and the tumultuous friendship that started? She got out immediately after seeing, making eye contact, and leaving, muttering things in the air. I sense told me I heard her. I heard the words. I saw her as well.

I have to prepare the text of "Tio Daniel" soon. I have to edit, proofread, revise, and amplify. I have to start from the top. I have to relax. I have to start from the beginning. I have about forty-seven pages of single-spaced prose. I have to concentrate. I have to finish this page. This is something I have to do. I have to keep writing. I have to publish it soon.
I keep reading *Look Homeward, Angel* by Tomas Wolfe.

The story is written to be published. I have to write it in one try. It has to be polished and done right. God bless Bella. St. Ita, pray for us. I need to be chill. I have to live. I have to go to Church. I have to listen to myself, and just chill. I have to listen.

Write your thoughts. God bless my mom, may she pray, and be safe. During the day, I would lay in bed, and hear the neighbors from next door talk. I could hear them. God bless Ruby. They're never going to arrest him again if he has good sex. Fight. Hear thoughts.

A car's engine roaring. Fuck me. Fuck me is a thought. Fuck em is a directive. Joyce Carol Oates deserves the Nobel Prize in Literature. God let Joyce win the Nobel. I have to write my thoughts. I have to stay still. I have to just chill. I have to write. St. Joseph, let me be a father with that girl. I need to have sex (with women, lots of them). I need to get a wife. I have thought long and hard about this. I have to be a father. I have to be a husband (by religion, state, or consummation). I have to be a teacher.

I have to stand-up. I have to just be one. I have to breathe. I have to not ignore my thoughts and be chill. I have to ignore my lonely thoughts (or, at least interporet them, think about them). I have to fight. I have to be me. I have to be me and no one else. I wish I did not smoke. I wish I could stop. God let me stop.

Joe- Part 2

When I lived on Cermak and Blue Island, I lived close to Joe's sister. I had seen a picture of her shown to me by Joe. I lived on the same block as hers. I saw her around the block. She was never alone, always accompanied. She was a good girl. I have to just be self. I have to sex (with the woman I meet, and the women I am attractive to, and the women who ioffer themselves to me). I have to offer myself as well. I have to make my announcement. I have to make my announcement that I am looking to get married (any type of way). I have to smoke now. I have to save two shirts and a polo.

Wlater Van Tilburg Clark in *The Ox-Bow Incident* writes, "when there's something bothering you that you can't do anything about, you always get sleepy" (219, New York: The Modern Library, 2001). I think you put your mind at rest when you can't control what you want to create. I was reading and then I stopped. I have to write again. I have to look for decisions that do not go against me. I have to write, and look for girls that I talk to. I have to keep talking to girls. I have to find Josephine.

I have to make peace with Nia. I have to breathe. I have to relax. I have to have sex. I need sex. I have to be a father. I have to figure out a way to pray. The book, the play, *The Winter's Tale* by William Shakespeare is ready to read. God bless Dori, may she pray, and be safe. 6/16/2022

I have to talk about my faithfully departed niece, Penny. She passed away under a year old. May God Rest Her Soul. She passed away when I was at work on my full-time shift. I was working my twelve-hour shift. I used to work from 7pm to 7am. I came home at around 9pm. I used to take the bus to Little Village and the Red Line, before that a Cermak bus. I used to clock in, check-in, at around 6:15 and then take a bus, a company bus, to the *taller*, a cup and manufacturing plant that was located in a suburb.

I used to clock-in, and then go pack boxes with sleeves of plastic cups. I then used to switch and take a break while another worker filled the station. I used to come back, and then work more to change statins. I then used to go to other stations, do physical labor, make pallets, stack boxes on pallets, wrap them, and move them with the pallet jack. I then walked around the warehouse looking for work. I fodun work walking around.

God bless Penny. Eternal Rest Grant Unto Her, and Let The Perpetual Light Shine Upon Her. Amen

I came home the day after with my bag over my shoulder. I did not want to write. I needed to live. I needed to understand. I came home to my mother's home. I came home to see my sister cradled on the couch. She had given me a call the night before in the early morning) on my way from work. I talked to her for a bit on the company bus.

I took the train and bus back and ran home. I went in to see my sister calm and collected. She wasn't crying. She wasn't standing. I sat next to her and cuddled her. I did not know how to feel.

I told her in the immense silence that engulfed us, "What happened?" I did not understand. I didn't think of the immense silence. I did not think this ws real. The torture that my sister went through including hte kids and Penny (May she Rest in Peace) is soemthing I did not fathom. I saw the house later on and was paused. I have to keep buying roses. I have to be in control. There's value in just progressing. There has got to be a way to write about my Grandma.

There's a picture of her wearing a blue suit. It's the only picture I personally had. May She Rest in Peace. I set it on fire today out of anger. God forgive me. I don't think I will doubt my faith in myself. I printed a picture of Penny (May She Rest in Peace). I dedicated my first book to her, a collection of short stories titled *Short Stories*.

My Grandma passed away in January. This is June. I have to know where and when I'm going to land. I just have to relax. I read something today about sexual fear. I have to conquer that. There's sex in CPS (Chicago Public Schools). There's rape int he bathrooms bny security guards and maintenance. St. Joseph, let me be a father. God keep Ruby safe at all times.

I have to keep buying roses. I have to be in control. There's value in just progressing. There has got to be a way to write about my Grandma. God bless two shirts and two ties. There's a good cause if I just learn to breathe. If I learn to be chill and progress. If I control my anger. I have to leave the ahrm behind. I have to leave everything that seems to be causing me harm, bad health, and self-doubt. I think sometimes doubt gets in the way. When we don't believe what we know is true. When we know that we all achieve what we have to. That is doubt. I think doubt is a form of faith. Doubt lets you know that faith is coming. Faith, a wholehearted belief in oneself and a Higher Being is an enormous thing. Doubt is the lack of faith, or the lack of belief in faith, is not a complete rejection of faith. Doubt can lead to faith once we encounter doubt. We have to control how we act. I think doubt is something that leads to something bigger. Through the thinking of doubt we might create a crevice that leads to light. I think doubt is pain, but it goes away. I think doubt will certainly lead to faith especially when conquering your doubt with thought, belief, and action. See what you believe, become what you receive.

I am desperate to know what went on. I have to believe I can achieve it. I have to be me. There's a lot of faithful departed souls who know they are gone, need prayer. Most connect the world with their minds. Most of their thoughts are with us, and are heard. Most of them have faith like my Father, Jesus Perea (Eternal Rest). I believe most have gone with faith. Some with pain. Some have lost sense of the world. Some had thoughts before leaving. Some prayed and saw the light. I believe those that need prayer should ask. I believe those that ask for prayer. I don't want to grow up to be an evil man. I know there is God. I know I have faith. I know I don't have to follow the wrong path. I know I have to follow my own. I know I am alive and can make my own decisions. I ask God to show me His path. I ask God to forgive the sins of my ancestors. I ask God to show me the way. I ask not to commit the same sins as them, not to commit the same mistakes, I ask God to help me carry this burden. I also ask God to let me have my mind. I ask God to keep all harm, all harmful people, and harmful vents away from me.

I ask God to keep all harmful pales, and thoughts away from me. I ask God to come back into my life. I ask God to show me the path. I ask God to have Mercy on me. I ask God to look in favor on me as I look to be a husband and father.

The Content Test is pushed back further. I have been on a binge the last couple of days. I have also been smoking weed non-stop. I pushed it back more than a month. I am now taking in July close to the date. I am getting my teaching license on August 1st, my Grandmother's birthday.

The Test is discombobulated, untrained, unwashed, unvarnished, unrestrained, it's a tool to measure your commitment, your desire, your willingness to live. It's a measurement tool to satisfy the state's crave for your knowledge. The test is a tool to measure your willingness to persevere, to sit still, to go onto the next question when you don't have the answer. The test is a measurement of your knowledge, of the knowledge they want to have. The test is an acknowledgement of that knowledge. The test is an acknowledgement that I know that knowledge and cause it for good.

The test is just a tool to measure what I know, what I need to know, and what I will know. I need to know what I need to know about the Content Test. I have to just go on and live my life how I want. I have to "let the Dead bury the dead," as the Bible states. I have to let my Grandmother go. I have to keep living. Jesus told one of his disciples to follow him and not to bury his dead, "Let the Dead bury the Dead," Jesus proclaimed. He then followed Jesus Christ. He also said don't plow and look back at your work to one discipline who wanted to turn back and check on his family. Jesus exclaimed to him, "No one who puts a hand to the plow and looks back is fit for the Kingdom of God" Luke 9.62. To me that means don't look back at your work. "Let the Dead bury their own Dead" in Luke 9:60 means don't worry about the dead, don't worship the dead, and don't fantasize about the dead. I will live until 89.

This is life. I have to live to 77. I have to live to 87. I have to just be me and live and breathe. I have to just live, breathe, and just be the best self I can. I have to read and read a lot.

I started a second book of the novel "Look Homeward, Angel" by Thomas Wolfe. This is the second time I have started the book. The first book is a first edition from the 20's and 30's. I have to find a journal to publish "Tio Daniel." I have to breathe and feel okay. I have to write as much as I can. I have to see my sister and the kids soon. I feel okay. I feel the world is in place. I feel a part missing. Mostly my mom and my sister. And also Miguel.

I have to keep writing about my Tio Daniel, my Grandmother, and my mom. I especially like to pray for my Grandma. She dies during the writing of this novel. I have to pray for my niece, Penny. She is an innocent.

My Tio Daniel is lost. My grandmother passed away recently. My mom, I have not seen in three days. My niece Penny passed away more than three ago. She was a baby. Her name was Penelope Chanel Vitela. Penelope Chanel Vitela. I have to keep praying. I have to keep giving peace to people. I have to keep finding peace with people. I have to read what I want to read. Right now I'm reading through Thomas Wolfe and *Look Homeward, Angel.* I got through about forty pages the first time.

Eliza. I have a first cousin named Eliza. She's cool. Eliza is also a character in *Look Homeward, Angel.* She is the wife. The husband drinks a lot. I have been through poverty. No, I am in poverty. I have not beaten poverty. There's also violence. There's tremendous violence that seems to evaporate after a bit.

There's tremendous violence that seems to evaporate after a bit. There's also jobs, businesses, that seem to fail, whores that seem to love, but are scared. In *Look Homeward, Anel* Gaunt and his son don't know how to love. There's also humans, humanity, and personhood. There's also intense scrutiny of everyone. Gaunt is always bickering with his wife in the novel.

Tengo que escribir en español mi primer idioma. Yo creo que mi mama no se siente bien. No la he visto en tres días. Hoy la vi. Le dije que una laptop iba a llegar al domicilio. Yo necesito que Ruby esté segura y fuera de peligro. Mi mama yo creo que voy hacer un maestro. Yo creo soy lo que soy. No vi a mi ahijada Jazzlyn.

Me siento mal que Gustavo el neighbor did not eat. Voy hacer un maestro otra vez en dias diaz. Mi internship va a empezar. Dios Bendiga. I gotta go back to English fo Coheed and Cambria. God bless my friend and her friend. Tengo que seguir El Espanol. In the song by T.I. "Dead and gone" the lyrics sing, the chorus in the end sings, "I turn my head to the East," eventually mentioning three directions. I don't write. I ask for wealth.

Chapter 39: Practice Test

There are not practice tests for the content test except one. Online, there is only one online practice test for the content test. There needs to be more reliable study materials for the test. There is no guidance. There is only one test, and it is a long one. The practice test is a good test. There are questions from previous tests in the study guide (practice test). THe practice test is a good test. I keep expecting study materials to be updated. There are no study materials outside of the test website that are current. Most, if not all, are for the TAP (Test of Academic Proficiency) with the writing sections and Math Section.

Today, I found out that Great-Grandmother died young. The mother of the grandfather died before my mother was born. My mother never met her grandmother (on her father's side). When my mom was born my grandfather was thirty-four. My great-grandmother was already gone.

The current study guide of the test is an old, outdated text. Before the test was minimized into a smaller test, the test was one long egregious. The test guides are outdated with questions from the old test (the TAP test). The content test was created a few years ago. It is now structured around your discipline. My discipline is ELA.

The pre test guides had the same questions. There is no new content to study except the questions in the practice test online. There are no private companies that offer a practice

Content Test. How does this relate to mom? I think I keep going back to the same practice as before to see my mom. Maybe, I am waiting to act. I think I think about my mom and the way I relate to her.

I think what I need to interpret, understand, and like is my past, but not relive it, renew the good aspects of it, and reject the past mistakes I've made, and of my ancestors. I need to live. I live to be married (and to someone I truly love, admore, and get along with). I don't need to be married to someone I will be judged over. God will judge me. I need to be a father like my father. I need to feel his soul. I need to be a grandfather like my grandfather. I need to be a husband (and be my own husband). No one showed me how. I will have to figure it out myself. I want to be my own husband. Again, my own husband.

God let me write. I need a new outline. A completely new line. I have to write about what's going on in my mind. Write your thoughts. My great grandmother has been on my mind lately. She lost her life for his son. Ironically, (God forgive me if I am wrong), her son, my grandfather, did not live a good life. Or, lived the best life he could. My mom, again, did not meet her paternal grandmother (Rest in Peace).

I don't know what to do. It seems I know and have to write. I have to do something to just type, and keep writing my novel. I have to stay strong and start studying for the Content Test again. I have to just breathe. I have not studied in a while. I am not seeing my mom regularly, but am just visiting sporadically. I visited yesterday, and left right away. I have to type all day today on a laptop. I have to breathe. I have to chill. I am currently reading Thomas Wolfe and *Look Homeward, Angel.* I am about 150 pages in.

I am about to write, and write well. I have to make an outline for our meeting tomorrow. I have to tell Dr. Zuisie what I know about the world, mostly that I think she did wrong by insulting, calling me and letting me know to fail. I think Dr. Hide did wrong by not responding. I think I will stay calm. Right now, I have a message from Dr. Zusie informing me that she reacted to my email and not responded. I have to do me. I have to listen, and stay still. I have to tell myself that I am okay, and willing to succeed. I am staying still and not moving. It seems my mind is okay, and I am listening. I have to stay still, learn, and do me. I have to just live, breathe, and be me. I have to pray, and be okay. I have to listen, and listen. I have to just stay still. I have to be okay.

I have to stay calm and just write. I have to know that I will persevere and just write. Have to just write. I have to write and be calm. I have to write about Tio Daniel. I have to know what to write, and how I feel. I have to know how to write. I have to write. I have to let go of the use of "just." I have to know I have to be me. I have to drink coffee. I have to look for clues about my heritage.

I have to know where I'm going. I have to know what is going on. My Tio Daniel is just the son of my grandfather, Rodrigo Haro, and Maria Santos Haro, my grandmother. Both Rest in Peace. My grandfather is the son of Jesus Haro and Mercedes Haro. That's the bloodline.

My Tio Daniel has direct descendants and relatives. He is the youngest son of three. (He has my Tio Jorge who changed his legal name to george Haro, and my Padrino Jose who has a large family).

He has three little sisters beginning with my mom, then my Tia Guille, and also my Tia Rosa who is the youngest woman. My Tio Daniel has direct descendants including his nephews, my brother, my sister and her kids, all my cousins, and me. He might have a son or daughter.

Today was a great day. I talked thoroughly to Dr. Hill. I was in contact with her. I also settled my case regarding my internship. It seems that I was confused. It seems that I was betrayed according to me. It seemed that was my feeling regarding my placement, and lack of a third week. It seemed I was misplaced by the department, or at least placed a week too short. I have to be comfortable at Dominican University.

I have to pray to St. Dominic and St. Clare. My mom;s patron saint (of her birthday). I have to keep teaching no matter what. I have to write my heart out. I have to just push and be studious. I have to make sure I do what I'm supposed to do. I have to just be me. There's something I have to do and that is write. I have to write and write. I don't think I can drink (and smoke) and persevere. I have to be sober. I have been reading Thomas Wolfe and *Look Homeward, Angel* . It is a trying story about family dysfunction. I have to understand the story, the characters, and the situation in the novel. I have to turn the page, and be me. I have to write and write. I have to finish my education.

The Content Test is an unmovable object. I have to opus harder. I have to think of me. I am going to gain more strength. I have to figure out how I will push with all my strength. I have to conquer the test, and push it hard until it's all the way to the top. Like Sysiphus. I have to gather strength, push with all my might, and go to the top. I have to figure out how the rock will be pushed. I have to push. The content has fallen before. I have picked it up again and again. I have gone down to the depths to pick it up, to pick up the rock, the Test, and have gathered strength, pushed it calmly, calmly, through the light. I have aged as I have pushed it up. IO have to find a way to go down and pick up the rock and pushed it back up. I have not studied for the test in a couple of weeks since I re-scheduled it. I have to find a way to grab the rock, push it around, and go to the top even if it falls down again.

I have to feel okay, feel strength, and push again. The Content Test has to be light. It's actually heavy. A heavy, unmovable object. At times it's a moveable object. It seems that this time, the rock, the Content Test, is something worth pushing. I have to know where I am going. The liquor store is not the place I have to go to. I have to stay still when the rock is heavy. And our strength is to push it a bit at a time. I have to just focus on the push, the slight push to tilt it forward. I have to keep calling mom. I have to keep calling and stepping up and walk myself to my mom.

Yo pienso que tengo que hacer el placer. (Maybe I have to have sex in my place.) There's a girl upstairs, who goes up to the third floor, and gets abused. Tengo que andar y disfrutar el dia. Yo pienso que tengo que tomar mas cafe. La nina, muchacha esta bella y tiene mucha sed y fe. Tenia un dress. Yo pienso que tenía que hablar y hice mal por no saludar. Tenia fe and tiene fe. Vive alado en la casa gray.

I had a friend a long time ago. I wrote a short piece of fiction a couple of years ago. It was love. It was betrayal. It was hardship together with hardship. I recently saw her again. I saw her with her mother this past weekend, Mother's Day weekend. I saw her mom light up. I saw her in shorts. I saw her dance.

I saw her aftera festival, the Randolph Festival. I also saw my neighbors that used to live on the bottom floor, a girl probably eighteen years old, pretty, who I fell in love with. She had pretty eyes, the same beautiful eyes. I also saw a girl at Osito's close to 26th Street whose name is Ashley. I saw her behind. I also saw another girl, her friend, who I fell in love with as well. I also met another girl, an artist, who was painting at the festival, Puerto Rican and beautiful. I met another female nurse who was praying with me. I also met many other girls at the festival.

Chapter 40: The OJ Incident and girls

There's an incident with OJ, orange juice. My roommate constantly chugs and swigs the OJ from the container. I have told him before to use a cup since we have to share. It's a bottle, caton, or gallon. It's made to be shared and poured. It's not a small bottle. It's supposed to be in the fridge. I think the act is an act of anger. I think he knows he is supposed to get a cup, but ignored his thought. He refuses to do what is right. Now no one has OJ.

I threw the OJ down the sink, and threw the bottle away. He has done it before. He has taken OJ to his room, and I have asked for it back. He refuses to respect respect. He refuses to do right, keep what is his, and not touch what is not his. He refuses to fit (he refuses to not do right) and refuses to avoid negligence. He refuses to avoid tragedy, and respects everyone else around him to fix his wrongs. He does not hold himself accountable, and wants everyone else to be accountable for his actions.

I think the only solution is to hold him accountable, or keep my OJ in my room. It will be warm, but oh well. I think it's not right to not do right. I'm not sure why he doesn't own OJ. Why doesn't he keep what's his? Or, get his own things. It seems there is a childish aspect to ti, kind of immature. I'm sure he looks around trying to figure out how to fix conflict, but runs into a bigger obstacle, or conflict. He might make the conflict bigger by running into it. I hope and pray to God he finds himself.

I had a great day. I have to publish *Tio Daniel*. I have to revise it and just publish it, and submit it. I have to tiem myself. I have to just do it, revise, rewrite, and find a journal. There's new material. I have to publish in a journal. God let me keep a reading journal for Thomas Wolfe and his novel, and keep track of one character. It's mostly content that I already read and reviewed. I have to get back together with Jay and just talk to her before publishing the novel.

I met a girl today at the library. Her name is Clare. She had a friend with her. She also had a guy friend who came in. I completed my homework at the library. I was at the Little Italy library right by UIC. I also saw other people, and another girl with gold.

I saw a kid with his dad, and a mom, and African-American mom. She is the housekeeper. I also saw a guard. I saw a dad with a little girl who looked adoptive. I also saw a black girl in pink. I saw a mother trying to get a book for her daughter. I saw another guy in gold. I saw a black woman in balck. I saw another woman trying to be calm and collected. I also saw a girl in church wearing similar clothes to Delani Adams. I saw a girl next to a gold girl. I also saw tables, a family (an Asian family) running around the parking lot. I saw another girl in front. I saw little girls trying to get books (white with blonde hair).

This past weekend I saw an Indian girl with booty shorts and a golden retriever, I also remember a girl from the hospital with blue clothing. I remember a girl from Vegas who was blonde as well. God bless.

I met a girl on the road. She was wearing brown pants. I called her "swanky pants" in my mind because sensualized her butt. I need to keep walking where I'm walking. I also need a haircut. I have to hold still, and just relax. I have to find my old friend Suli (or, as she was known, Ulce) though it will be painful. I also have to find my old friend Naydi. I have to know she's okay. I have to keep saying hi. I have to make peace with her. She sent a bunch of messages on Facebook and then told me to contact her on another messaging app. We never exchanged numbers. I have to know where she's at. I have to get her a pair of glasses. I have to get myself a pair of glasses as well. I have to make peace with her asap. She's a good friend, but everyone is envious, jealous, and bed ridden. Not able to see the light. Envy is extreme jealousy of what someone else has. But don;t lose what you have by attaining what everyone else has. The Lord knows this is our world.

I'm sure I have to keep track of a character. I'm sure I have to keep track of Eugene in *Look Homeward, Angel* by Thomas Wolfe. I have to keep track of my reading journal. The character seems to be taking a trip with his friends, his mother, and his two girls. It seems he not looking for grace, but is spending the family money. There's a mom, Eliza, (there was also a girl Elizabeth) who was in the novel. She was a love interest.

I have to know the main character. There's a way for the character to come alive. I have to know where Eugene is at all times. There's a way to pray with the text. I know the text. Eugen is the main character trying to live. The novel is a love novel, a family saga. It seems Thomas Wolfe worked hard on it, and developed it fully. The family saga will come together at the end. The novel has to end. I have to read it completely.

My Tio Daniel was the son of my Grandmother. He was the third son of her marriage to Rodrigo Haro, my Grandfather. He was / is lost. I never met him. Although, there was a picture of him (which my mother always asked for). I only got a glimpse of it. I only got a glimpse of it when my Grandma pulled it off the pantry door. She kept it there for safekeeping. My mom always wanted the picture. She never wanted to forget him. My mom always talked about him as if (we did) they (whoever they is) did something bad (horrible) for him. It was good of my mother to (be with him) remember him. She struggled through her pain. She struggled because of his absence. I never understood why he got lost. I never understood why he got lost. I never understood why they never looked for him. I always thought they could find him opening a case on the Cristina show. I was confused.

Maybe my novel is about sex. Roe v. Wade was turned back today.

This is a sentence.

Chapter 41: New Chapter

Today, I was removed (once again) from teaching. I was removed because of a conflict of interest. I was fired because of racism. I was fired because of sexism against men. I was fired because I could not prove that I wanted someone else besides myself. I was let go because I could get along with my supervisor. I was fired because I wanted to teach. I was removed because I couldn't explain that I was in prayer. I could not explain that I wanted to teach. The program at Dominican University has ended. The program ended fast. I wish she would have understood. I wish I could teach in the memory of my Grandmother. Or, maybe I have to live my own life, follow my own path, and be who I want to be. Maybe, I have to be a professor. Or, maybe I have to stop comparing myself to others. Maybe, I have to stop thinking of the worse.

There is a professor that kept calling my phone. Shebombarded my phone three times. She told me once before admissions that I was not deemed worthy of attending. She also told me before the internshi, when I was already admitted, God don't let me touch my money except for the baptism. God let me spend all my money on the baptism. God let me write. The professor also talked to me yesterday, and told me that I needed to think. She told me that she was in a panic attack and that she did not want to be "hesitant." She said she tired of being hesitant and needed to send emails. She also said I could not teach. She told me to not try. She also had things to say that she did not say,. Mostly, she could not say why she was calling or acting. She could not tell me why she sent the text outlining her refusal to let me teach. Do I need permission? I think God gave me permission to write and teach. I might have to teach on a different level, college or university. It's going to take time though. I think most likely I will get into another program soon. I think she has stress issues. I think she practices the sin of envy. Immensely, I think I have the power to abandon her to her own destruction. I have to rebuild. I have to get another MAster's Ihave to look for another program.

I have to apply soon. I have to pay my fee for my online MA in Creative Writing from Eastern Illinois University soon. I have to find out if I can still apply, or if the deadline has passed. I have to keep working. I have to know I'm a writer then a teacher. I have to write and not look back. I have to keep writing. I have to hold on to dear life. I have to be still. I have to keep on trying. I have to write. I have to be an expert in writing and reading. I have to read. I will read Philip K. Dick next. I will read *Divine Invasion*. I have to understand the novel before I read it. I have to know the novel and vision he put forward. I think the novel is about God. I think the novel is about his own salvation. From what I have read, this is his own revelation. This is his spiritual journey. This is his own revelation of Heaven. I have to know what Philip K. Dick was going through at the time of his writing.

I came to the conclusion that I can be a Substitute Teacher at Chicago Public Schools. I can still persevere. I can move on from bad people. I can be productive and still be good people and seek good people. I have to be still. I have to be okay. I have to keep on constructing. I can also a CHicago Police officer or a firemen. Or, almost anything., I can teach. I don;t have to be anything other than the teaching thing.

I don't have be anyone other than the writing thing. I have to be a writer first. If I am not a writer, I can't be a teacher. I have to write in order to teach writing. I have to teach as well. If I would ask my mom for Wisdom she would tell me to keep on teaching, She would also tell me to be a father. I have to pray for my father. May God Grant His Soul Peace and May God Grant Him Rest. God let me be a father. I have to keep looking for what I want.

Dr. McD. crossed a lot of boundaries. Here are the boundaries I refuse others to cross:

Name-Calling. Demeaning language. "You can't" language. Time boundaries. Professional boundaries (keeping me from doing my work). Personal boundaries (keeping, isolating, or demeaning others to not be around me). Cutting off a support system. Isolation. Telling people to not be around me. Physical Boundaries (being around my space). Emotional Boundaries (making others feel unsafe when using words, hurting others knowingly, stratign an argument). These are boundaries that can't be crossed. And that have to be acknowledged. I need to establish boundaries with my mom. I need to establish career boundaries.

Chapter 42: Substitute Teaching Protocol

I have applied for a substitute before. I will interview and substitute in the Fall again. I have to be in the classroom and teach lesson plans. I have to substitute anyway I can. I have to get in a classroom. I have to prove that I can teach and persevere. There is a process for teaching. I have to pass that process. I have to be a success. I have to be a successful substitute.

I have to have my interview for substitute teaching. I have to have the third interview in person or online. I have to think of the other interviews and what went well. I will interview soon. I have to log on or go to an interview in a school. The last in-person interview was at a school in the South close to Cermak Rd. The other interview two years later was online with a principal that wanted to leave her address.

I have to use my substitute license.that I acquired a couple years ago. I had my first interview at a school in the South. I entered the building by the entrance and was lost. I saw a table with my name on sheets of paper. There was a volunteer signing people in for interviews. I signed in and was confused. I didn't know where to go. I walked around the building. I could not find it. I kept telling myself that I was in the wrong building. I took the doors to the gym. I was in a huge gym. I saw tables, and was lead to one. I saw a principal, African-American, in a table and she invited me to seat. I had a great interview. She told me to keep teaching. She passed the interview. I passed the interview. I passed it by talking about myself. I told her I wanted to teach to help. I told her how I know to teach. I told her I knew my discipline to each. I told her I wanted to teach in and for the community I grew up in. I told her I know interdisciplinary teaching methods. I knew how to handle a classroom. I was granted the interview. I wore my suit. I walked out and did not know where to go. I was elated. I called my mom to tell her that i had passed the interview. I had an incredible interview. I did not think I was doing anything. The interview was hard to get to. I did not know where I was. I was lost along the way. I took the green line and then a bus to the high school. I could have walked. I thought the building was another building.

I kept on walking home to the North after my interview. I think I was living in the Nest. I thought i Was going to teach immediately after interview. I did not pay off my debt to the City. I also had an outdated TB test. I had to do these two things asap. I did not do any of them, but instead kept writing and trying to call my mom. I went ahead and waited to act. I know I had to save a thousand. I kept on going to school.

I went to the Human Resources department two weeks later. I was told to wait and pay off my debt. It was a highlighted office building with fluorescent lights. It looked like a cubicle, a large cubicle with partitions with departments. It looked like a warehouse from the outside. A trailer.

The second interview was online. The second interview I got after I left Northeastern, the initial MAT program. I logged on and was prepared. I took noted before the interview. I took notes on the usual interview questions. Tell me a time when you had to work through trouble? Tell me a time when you had to work with a co-worker who you did not like? Tell me a time when you had to work through conflict? I also looked up the usual questions about teaching that I was going to be asked. I looked up how to handle to a classroom. I looked up how to teach. I looked up the usual teaching questions that I would be asked. I then wrote down the questions and answers to the questions. I prayed. I write down what I knew I needed to know and say. I logged on and said hi. I was dressed up. I told the Principal, who lived in the South, who I was. She was African-Americann and she told me to stay with her.

I went ahead with the interview. She asked me about my history, I gave her the usual speech about my education, work, and teaching experience. I told her I had been a teacher before. I told her I had been a Chicago Public School educator before. I told her I needed to just breathe. I told her I needed to be back in the classroom. I was in my Roger's Park apartment. I had not been to a classroom in a while. This was after I had removed myself from student teaching,.I was ready to breathe.

I saw the Principal in her home office. I saw her wearing dressed clothes, I think she was wearing red, or brown. I looked into her eyes and knew she wanted to get out of her address. I knew she was praying with me.

The third interview I will have to have soon. THis is July 8th when I'm writing this. It's 2022. I will have to prove how to teach, and how I teach. I will have to show how I teach, what I teach, and why. I have to teach and teach, and teach. I have to have the interview soon. I have to keep teaching. I have to do everything that I did in the first two interviews. I have pass the interview with flying colors. I have to do everything that I did in those two interview. I have to pass the interview in person opr online. I think I will have an okay interview. I think I will have to think about what I need from teaching. I think I am asking God for wealth. I don't think my life, or what I am asking, and my prayers are jokes. I don't think my dreams and those of my family are jokes. I don't think I should be losing my faith. I think I should be where I need to be. I think I should visualize where I need to go and be there. I think I have to be myself teaching in Little Village. I think I will pass it. I think I will be n a classroom again. I think I have to show myself that I will persevere. I think I have to get more experience and possibly get another degree, and join another alternative licensure program. I will have to get writing. I will get an MA in english with a Creative Writing emphasis soon. I will have to keep writing. I will show other people my writing.

I have started reading Philip K. Dick and his novel *The Divine Invasion*. I am a couple of pages in. The book is about finding God. The book is about his family. In the novel, the protagonist seems to care about his significant other. They don't have sustainables. There is a ffodman that he goes to and is always talking about.

I have to find a way to teach again even if for one class or day. I have to find a way to get a Masters or work with my Bachelor's in schools. I have to just be me. I have to teach in community colleges and high schools and later in universities. I have to stay still. I have to substitute quick. I have to think of myself and get pozole from my mom or a restaurant in Little Village, or La Villita. I have to live in Little Village while being a public school teacher, getting my Master's, and writing my heart out. I have to be a father in Little Village.

I have been reading Philip K. Dick and his novel *Divine Invasion*. It's about writing and being a writer. It's about struggles. It's about love. Klts' about God and faith. It's about philosophy and how we know. It's about how we know ourselves, the world, and God. It;s about how we know ourselves and others. Mostly, how we know the world.

There is a girl named Zina in the novel. In *The Divine Invasion* by Philip K. Dick she seems to be the mother although it's not certain. There is another girl, Rabies, she is the mother of Emmanuel. There is Hash who seems to be a mentor. Elias, named after the Prophet Elijah, is the father of Emmanuel (or so it seems).

I have to pray. I have to pray for myself and ELslie. I have to keep praying. She's a good person. She is my girl. I think I will keep dating her. The objective world seems . . .I have to know what objective means. I have to know what is in vape. I have to understand to understand. I have to keep praying. I have to pray for her family. St. Thomas Aquinas, pray for us. I have to know that Leslie is alright.

I met a girl tonight. I'm sure she got raped liekd every other woman I try to love. I'm sure I'll just move on. I'm sure I'll just meet another girl. It seems fruitful to be alive. I guess I just have to live and let live. I have to look around for God and know I'm alright. I'm with God and no one else.

I have to find a way to not drink today, or at least not drink a lot. I have to stand still and stand my ground. I have to look for what I want. I have to look for more love and non-revenge. I have to look for a way to not go insane (do the same things twice and expect different results) and crazy (which means not listening to my mind and questioning my mind). RIght now, my mind's telling me to drink a beer with pina flavor. Or, at least my mind that I had drink the beer earlier. I guess I had to protect myself from harm.

I just have to keep myself safe. I have to know what to do when I have to do it. I have to do everything I can to make a salary, and a middle-class salary, 45K to 50K or above sounds right. Like the Chicago Police Department. I am scheduled to take the third test in July.

I did not drink the beer. I bought the beer. In addition to three others. I bought a orange flavored beer and a Michelada, tomato flavor, with the pina beer. I threw out the pina beer down the drain. I also did not drink the Michelada, tomato falover, one. My roommate, who I am not sure is a friend or wants to become a friend, drank it. I guess he wants to become an enemy which is not great. Which is someone I do not want.

I am not sure where the novel is supposed to go. It could end in a tragedy. A tragedy needs a love story. The love story ends in death. One of the two lovers gets killed or both. The novel could also end in a comedy. It could end in a marriage, a consummation, a legal marriage, or ceremony. Thai novel most likely needs other elements. The novel needs more plot. The plot revolves around teaching. The novel needs a clmax, a conflict, a denouement and resolution. The novel could also be in its denouement. The novel could also be non-confrontational. The novel could also be calling for more action. The action has to follow the elements of plot, the curve that has the elements of plot. At the same time, I don't have to follow that diagram, but only write what the novel asks of me. Ithink I will keep writing the novel. The novel has to be written one way or another. I have to write what I have to write. This nove is neither or either tragic or comedic. It has elements of both. I have to decide.

There is a priest in *The Divine Invasion* by Philip K. Dick. He is a cardinal in a church united by Christians and Jews. I have been thinking lately of what to do with my EIU app. I have been thinking that I have to stay still and not do anything. I have to not think. The cardinal has a whore in the novel. I have to understand the novel from the Cardinal's point of view although the novel is in a third person point of view. I have to keep thinking of the cardinal and the girl from Apsi. Alpha Psi Lambda is my fraternity. I have to think of them and their friendship. I have to think of what to do and what to say. I have to think of what to say to the big ex, who I don't think I will see much. I went to Vegas with the girl from A-Psi. I have to think of her and her brother. She seems nice in a dress. She has a big butt. I have to think of myself and no one else. I have to think of how to survive. I have to think of myself. I have to persevere. I don't have to be revered. I have to evere. Evere is a word that is not underlined in my Google doc folder. I have to know the word.

This novel is about my Grandmother (Eternal Rest and Let the Perpetual Light Shine Upon Her). She shooed me away from her. A girl that sells clothes with her mom on 26th St. also shooed me away when I told, "You're pretty."

I have to let go of pain. I have to let myself go and not think if I'm doing wrong if I know I'm following my heart. I have to know what I have to write. I have to know thyself like the great writer once told. I have to look for what I need. I have to find what I seek. I have to know if I will persevere. I will. The novel has to be of comfort. I have to know what I am writing. I have to know that there needs to be more characters. The main characters are me and my mom.

I am calling my mom everyday. I am not visiting my mom everyday. I visited her about two weeks ago. I am still with my mom. The Content Test was the struggle I had to overcome. The Content Test was the rock I had to push up. I have let go of the rock. It's all the way down. I have to pick it up eventually. What if I pickup another rock? I don't think that's how life works. My life is not perfect. I have to talk about other people in my life. Like Miguel.

He is my big brother. He is the oldest, my mom's first, and he goes to Exchange (my home) a lot. My mom has never kicked him out. I am not sure where I am going with this. My brother was the one that out me through college. I have to give him props for working a lot. I have to join him and rejoin him. He graduated first. He has to keep seeing my mom. He has the semblance of a king. I have to keep on writing. Miguel is a saint. Miguel goes to Exchange almost everyday. Miguel goes to Exchange when he wants. I think its awesome. Miguel ahs to understand that he needs to be in Exchange. I think i have to be with my mom. Miguel has to become a saint. I have to be by his side.

St. Francis de Sales bless my writing. Amen.

It seems I have to edit my novel immensely. I have to keep on revising. I have look f or last minute details to add. The novel is written although it needs a resolution. What will happen? My mom has to tell me what will go on. I have to know the actual COntent Test was not passed, but can be passed. I have to know that I will pass it eventually if I want, or do I just move on? Is the CPD test the new Content Test? I am sure I will have to pick it back up like Sysiphus. I have to pick up the rock again. I have to finish writing. There needs to be plots. If i write Dr. McDonough can fuck off? Is that offensive? If I say bless her. That's bette. I have to look for clues about what I have to write. Do I act superhuman? Do I write about fantasies, flying tables, angels in garages, the iceman? Rest in Peace.

I hate life. Look it up in The Holy Bible.

St. Francis de Sales bless my writing. Amen.

I have to finish this novel. My next step is to apply and get into the MA program in creative writing at EIU. Eastern Illinois is where Tony Romo went. I have to keep praying for them. I have to turn in my application with a full writing sample, statement of purpose, and curriculum vita. I have to finish *The Divine Invasion* by Philip K. Dick.

St. Francis de Sales bless my writing. Amen.

My dad, Jesus Perea, is from Zacatecas.

My Tio Daniel is from Zacatecas along with the rest of the Haro and Gonzalez clan.

My dad is Jalisco. Jalisco might mean a sense of fortitude. Jalisco might also mean a sense of pride, of achievement, and of control. I admire my dad. Eternal Rest Grant Unto Him and Let the Perpetual Light Shine Upon Him. Amen. My mind is alteright.

My mom is Jalisco. My dad married Jalisco. My dad is Zacatecas.

St. Francis de Sales bless my writing. Amen.

There is conflict in my apartment. Non-stop conflict and bickering and huge silence. The novel has to come to a conclusion. Is this novel about teaching? I think I already interpreted this. Yes and now. The future of my teaching career relies on my future endeavors. My teaching career will go on. I have to study for the CPD test as well. I will sib. I will become a substitute. I have to teach to create what I want to create. This novel is already more than 200 pages long. I have to know where it is headed. I have to pay off what I owe the City of Chicago in order to work for the City of Chicago. I have to know what is missing from teaching. If I am going to teach on a part-time basis after I get my Master's I will have to know how to teach. Again, If i become a Chicago Police Officer I will still have to know how to teach. Maybe, I'll become a part-time City College professor.

St. Francis de Sales bless my writing. Amen.

I have to earn my way into this writership. I have to earn by writing my way into this writer's world. I have to know who I am trying to emulate. I am trying to emulate great American writers like Philip Roth, John Updike, and Joyce Carol Oates and old writers like Philip K. Dick and Latino and LAtin American writers like Junot Diaz and Garcia Gabriel Marquez. Maybe this is the only way. Constant writing. Constant bickering with self. Constant turmoil. I guess the dark can sometimes not be alright. But if you get out of the cave of darkness there is light. Just get out. Remove yourself. See Light again. God bless the band. I have to pray.

Joyce Carol Oates had a character like herself. They are the protagonists of her novels. I admire her character Jesse Vogel and his will to survive. Joyce Carol Oates calls them survivors. There is a story of a woman who goes from party to party and does not get picked up by her would-be-lover at a party and walks home calling her real boyfriend. She thinks about their sex. These walks. I've taken these walks. "Lurk" Gwendolyn Brooks used. I am looking for what I need to find. I have walked. I don't have to fall. I have to walk on. I have to stand tall. I have to listen. There's a chance I might be okay. I have to stop weed to have sex.

I have not have sex ye tin Littel Village. I have met women, girls. I'll have sex soon. God bless us.

St. Francis de Sales bless my writing. Amen.

There are many plots in *The Divine Invasion* by Philip K. Dick. The latestone involves a cryogenic sleep by one of the characters. My thoughts are that the author always wanted this sort of state. He was in a similar state when he passed away. I wonder if we can write our own future? Can we write our way into history? I hope all this is for the greater God. I hope to understand. I hope to make sense of this duality. The need to fulfill prophecies in text and the need to live our lives through texts. How do we know what is going to happen to us without writing it? And how does that writing control us? If I say I am going to eat a pancake today, most likely I am. If ai write it I am. But how does me writing that declarative sentence control the act. I am going to eat a pancake today. What happens if I don't? What is God telling us?

I am trying to write what I need to write. I think my mom has to be in contact. I think I will have a better life. I will also spend time in the land that God promised me and that she gave me together with my dad. I think I will spend time in South Chicago eventually. I have to do something to follow my path. I think I will have a long life. I have to live life. I have to listen to more Kendrick Lamar.

St. Francis de Sales bless my writing. Amen.

God bless the mother let her be at home with her husband and daughter. Amen. I have to figure out what I am writing. I have to put the story in order. I have to make The COntent Test a priority. I have to know what is going to happen with teaching. The novel is about teaching and The Content Test. I no longer have to take the Content Test from The Illinois State Board of Education (ISBE). I got dropped again from teaching. I have to get my Master's to start teaching and have a chance at a Ph.D. I then will teach. I have to teach. I have been watching porn lately. I watched poirn all day today, yesterday, and the night before. I have to have real sex. God let me be a father in a year. The Content Test was a predicament of my proclivity to teach. The sentence before made no sense to me. The Content Test was required for the attainment of a teaching license.

I will now become a Chicago Police Department officer.

The End

Acknowledgements

I'd like to thank my mom, Abelina Haro. I'd also like to thank my dad, Jesus Perea, for giving me life. I would also like to thank my Grandmother who passed away in January of 2022 during the writing of this book. Thank you for showing me grace, fortitude, and patience. I'd liek to thank my sister Fabiola Perea. I would also like to thank my niece, Penny, for the love she showed me. I would also like to thank my goddaughter Jazzlyn for allowing me to be her guide through life. I'd also like to thank my nephew Angel Vitela and allowing me to show him how to play guitar. I'd like to thank my oldest nephew Daniel Perea, my niece Esmeralda Vitela, and my baby nephew Guillermo Vitela Jr. God bless you all. I would also like to thank my brother Miguel Campos for being with my mother.

Thanks to Amazon for helping me publish this, and to Jeff Bezos, and all the people behind the company who will help me publish, approve, and live with my art.

Thanks. God bless.